A Death in Dulcinea

a novel

by

Laramee Douglas

Alligator Tree Press
Victoria, Texas

This is a work of fiction. Names, characters, places, and incidents either are the products of the author's imagination or are used fictitiously. Any resemblance to actual events, locales, organizations or persons, living or dead, is entirely coincidental and beyond the intent of either the author or the publisher.

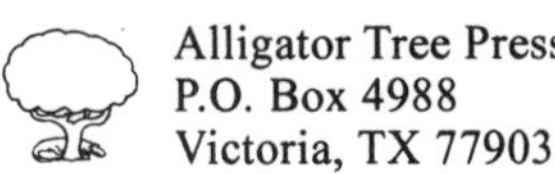

Alligator Tree Press
P.O. Box 4988
Victoria, TX 77903

Publisher's Cataloging-in-Publication
(Provided by Quality Books, Inc.)

Douglas, Laramee.
A death in Dulcinea : a novel / by Laramee Douglas.
— 1st ed.
p. cm.
ISBN 0-9713430-2-0

1. Murder—Fiction. 2. School librarians—Fiction.
3. Texas—Fiction. I. Title.

PS3604.O926D43 2005 813'.6
QBI05-800225

Printed in the United States of America

10 9 8 7 6 5 4 3 2 1

For the students and staff
of Profit High

ACKNOWLEDGMENTS

Thanks to:

Chief Tim Braaten for explaining the basics of criminal investigation and for reading the final draft.

Dr. Robert Harvey for answering questions about asthma and its treatment and for having your radio tuned to KVRT.

Maestro Darryl One for taking time out of your busy schedule to discuss the symphony, composers, and Harley-riding conductors.

Fan Chu Wu (Wu Fan Chu) for lessons in Mandarin and Chinese mothers-in-law.

Melanie Melançon for trying to catch all of your dear, old grandma's punctuation and grammar mistakes. I love you.

Adela Bump and Andie Carmona for Spanish lessons.

Patti Wilkinson for suggestions on early drafts. I miss you.

Patsy Brown, Sue Flanagan, Janet Kent, and Carol Zeplin for your friendship, suggestions, and enthusiasm for *A Death in Dulcinea* and/or *Dancing at the Shoulder of the Bull.*

Audrey Ellison for being my mom.

A *special thanks* to my husband Ted for your love and support.

A note: any errors appearing in this book are due to my own negligence rather than from information provided by these fine folks.

Chapter One

We live in The Great State of Texas, where motorcyclists have the God-given right to scrape up the pavement with their unhelmeted heads, where Grandma carries a .357 Magnum in her glove box, and where distance is measured in time.

My best friend Ariana and I had made the 125 miles in less than an hour and a half, and that included a bathroom break. Ariana wants all the horses running when she drives, so her Cadillac Escalade had all 345 lathered by the time we reached Austin. We were on a quest to find a gown for her to wear to a gala benefiting the construction of the new Performing Arts Center being held the following evening.

"Did Willemina find a photographer?" I asked.

Our good friend Willemina Henry is co-chairing the benefit with Ariana. They make a great pair. Ariana is great with details. If she had been at the Alamo, Bowie, Crockett, Seguin, and the rest of the troops would have been decked out in coordinating outfits, armed to the teeth, and possessed contingency plans for anything Santa Anna could have ever thrown at them.

Willemina moves people. She can talk you into sprinkling cactus spines on fried fire ants and convince you it's the most delicious dish you've ever eaten.

She and her husband, Richard, are outstanding patrons of the arts in Dulcinea. Richard is a plastic surgeon whose business is bursting at the seams because he takes in a lot of seams on the obese.

Willemina is a super organizer. Since most of their children have grown up and moved away, Willi has put her talents to use on the boards of the Dulcinea Performing Arts Council, the Dulcinea African American Chamber of Commerce, the Dulcinea Museum Association, the Dulcinea Medical Auxiliary, and numerous other organizations.

Together, we three friends are multilingual. Ariana is fluent in Spanish. Willi is fluent in French. I am fluent in Southern.

"You'll never guess who she got to handle the portraits," Ariana said. "Gary Nathe."

A wave of nausea hit me. "Oh, oh. *Bug guts,*" I said.

Ariana swerved into the nearest parking lot, slammed on the brakes, and threw the gearshift to PARK. Without looking at me, she said, "I hate when you say that!"

"I can't help it."

And I really can't. *Bug guts* is a feeling I get. This is what it's like. Imagine there's a great, big, ugly bug—like a giant cockroach—scurrying across your kitchen floor. So you reach out with your foot and step on it and hear it crunch and feel it squish nasty bug guts all over your clean floor and the sole of your shoe. You know how your stomach and throat involuntarily constrict at the thought? Well, that's the feeling I get when something bad is going to happen.

As much as she hates to hear it, over the years, Ariana has learned to trust my feelings. She turned to face me. "Is it the benefit? We don't need anything bad happening at the benefit. Tell me it's not the benefit."

"It's the benefit."

She pounded on the steering wheel. "I told you not to tell me!" Her frustration spent, she asked, "What's going to happen?"

"I don't know," I said. "I just got *bug guts* when you said Gary's name. But I don't think it's about Gary. I think it's about Claire." Gary Nathe is a very talented local photographer. Claire is his wife. She owns an interior decorating business. Gary is Mahatma Gandhi with a camera. Claire is Idi Amin wrapped in wallpaper samples.

"What about Claire?" Ariana asked flatly.

"I don't know. I don't get visions. I just get feelings."

"I *hate* that," she said. "Your ESP could be a little more specific."

"I don't have ESP," I said. "I just have sensitive senses."

"Whatever. I wish your senses could tell me *what* is going to happen. *How bad* is it going to be? *When* is it going to happen? Then I could be ready for it."

The trouble with demonstrating a talent other people haven't developed is that others look at you like you're weird and run for the hills, or they want you to give them a detailed read-out of the future, which I cannot do. Reactions like the one Ariana was exhibiting is why I keep this aspect of my personality quiet. Only Ariana, my husband, and my two children are aware of this trait. Thurman prefers to ignore it. Ariana wants me to turn it on and off like a spigot.

"Sorry," I said.

The hurt must have been evident because Ariana apologized. "I shouldn't have overreacted. It's just that we've worked so hard for all these months to have a successful benefit. We don't need Claire Nathe ruining it."

She sighed, then shifted into gear and carefully pulled back onto the street. We drove in silence for a few miles before she said, "Truthfully, I've been a bit apprehensive since Willi informed me Gary would be taking the pictures. He does a beautiful job, but I can't stand *la bruja* since I had that run-in with her last year."

"At the Lung Association benefit?"

"Yes. She made *such a scene* about not being recognized in the programs for the time she put in decorating the powder room."

"Claire's not really a witch," I said. "But she was a bit demanding."

"Demanding? I'd say! Claire *Nasty* wanted to be paid for her time and talent—what little she has—and that was after *she* had come to *me* and volunteered to help out," Ariana said. "She insisted on being listed as a major contributor even though she contributed no money *and* the committee reimbursed her for the supplies she'd used. Willemina made it very clear to her that if the rest of us were recognized for our time, we'd all be listed as *Premier Contributors."* Ariana took her hands off the wheel long enough to make little quote signs with her fingers. "Her name was already on the program under *Volunteers*. It really ticked me off when I had to get the commercial printer to run a program insert at the last minute to thank Claire's Concepts."

"You didn't have much choice. She threatened to strip the place bare if you didn't," I reminded her. "I don't understand why Willi would want to deal with her again."

"She said Gary handled the photographs at the Diabetes Fun Run and everything went off without a hitch. Of course, Claire was out of town for that event. Willi said if anything comes up *con la bruja,* she'll handle it." Ariana grew thoughtful. "To be on the safe side, maybe we should line up a last minute replacement. Wait a minute," she said suddenly.

"Maybe it's not really *bug guts*. Maybe you were on my wavelength and picked up on how I was feeling."

"Maybe," I said, trying to sound positive for her sake. "Or maybe my mind jumped from Gary to Claire and to how she acted at the Lung Association benefit. It could be just a bad memory."

"That's it," Ariana said hopefully.

But no matter how hard I wished, the feeling had nothing to do with past events. Of that I was certain. It definitely had to do with Claire Nathe. It had to do with the Performing Arts Center fund raiser. And it had to do with something very unpleasant lurking on the horizon.

Chapter Two

"What do you think about this one?" Ariana asked, removing an evening dress from the rack and holding it at arm's length. Tiny crystal beads shimmered on lavender jacquard.

"Gorgeous," I said.

"Hmmm." She turned the hanger to look at one side then the other. "I have one similar to it at home." She stuck it back on the rack.

Of course she did. Ariana is a former fashion model, which is why at the age of forty-nine she's still a size six, and why there were three Saks Fifth Avenue saleswomen hovering close by. I was certain, at any minute, they would surround Ariana and start begging for autographs.

When we first arrived in the after-five department, they glanced my way, determined I was not worth waiting on, and fell all over Ariana, which was very perceptive on their part. I guess the Dollar General bags I carried gave me away.

I am not a former fashion model. I am Darby Matheson, a former school librarian, and the last time I wore a size six, I also wore pigtails and played jacks on the sidewalk. I tried to get down to a size ten once, but the diet caused my fingernails to break, and my hair looked like a hairball coughed up by one of my cats; so for health reasons, I keep my weight hovering around one-sixty. On my five-foot frame that makes me just a tad on the non-svelte side.

I leaned against a rack of navy silk slacks. "I don't know why you had to wait this late to find something to wear. It's really not like you."

She sent me a patronizing look across the top of the rack. "Shopping at the last minute was not plan A."

"You could have worn something already in your closet."

"Now *that's* really not like me." She turned and walked to a rack of black dresses.

"You probably have twenty little black dresses now. You don't need twenty-one."

"They're all different."

I rolled my eyes heavenward. "Puleeease."

We had other stops to make, and if we were going to get out of the store by midnight, I was going to have to take charge. I searched the display along the back wall. "There it is," I said, pointing to a forest green, floor-length gown. "That is your color." I made a bee-line for the dress, but one of the salesladies beat me to it. Her name tag read: *Gladys Knight.* The other clerks must have been the Pips.

I wanted to wrench the dress away from Gladys and check the price. She seemed to be reading my mind, because I received one of those if-you-have-to-ask-you-can't-afford-it looks. I retorted with a neither-can-you smile.

Gladys turned with adulation to Ariana. "Your friend is so right, Ariana." She gasped, looking surprised and embarrassed at her own brashness. Trying to recover from the *faux pas,* she asked, "May I call you Ariana?"

Ariana smiled as she joined us. "Of course."

Most people didn't have a clue to her last name since she had modeled under the single moniker "Ariana". She didn't have to look at the price tag, but did, decided the gown was worth it, and disappeared into the dressing room with the saleswoman close at her heels.

I waited until the Pips had gotten busy elsewhere then peeked at the tag on the same dress in a size two. $3,500.00! Crime-o-nee! I could make the dress for a fraction of that. A very small fraction. Which is exactly what I do when I need a formal on those oh-so-many occasions—like, every five or ten years.

Since Willi and Ariana had saddled me with the title "Decorations Coordinator"—a highfalutin term for their lackey—I, too, was attending the benefit, so my recently homemade dress awaited its debut into society from a peg on my closet door.

Ariana needs formals much more often than I and can afford them—now—unlike when she was in college. That's where we met. I'd just moved into my dorm room and was still arranging things when my new roommate appeared in the open doorway. She was one of the tallest girls I'd ever seen. I was sure she was six feet or would have been if she'd stood up straight. But when she first came to College Station as a freshman, she was burdened with shyness and carried herself like a whipped pup, probably because of all the teasing she got from being the tallest girl in school and one of the few Mexican American kids growing up in the mostly white town of Cut and Shoot, Texas.

Ariana had no idea she was beautiful. Smart—yes. It was an academic scholarship that got her to A&M. Beautiful— no. So, I took it upon myself to make her my project and help her gain a little self-esteem.

I spent my first two years in school pouring over *Vogue,*

Cosmo, and *Mademoiselle,* clipping and pasting articles to Ariana's wall. She spent those years trying to shove calculus down my throat. When the makeup counters at Dillards had free makeup sessions, I'd haul Ariana to the mall and get our faces done. She would drag me kicking and screaming to math tutoring. I talked her into modeling at the mall's fall and spring fashion shows. She talked me into taking chemistry. I did my job *too well.* Not with chemistry, with Ariana.

At the end of our sophomore year, while waiting tables at The Dixie Chicken, Ariana was discovered by a modeling agent who was in town to see her nephew graduate. The agent's offer was a once-in-a-lifetime opportunity, and we both knew it. It took very little encouragement from me for Ariana to pack everything up and head to New York.

And as soon as I was out from under the scrutiny of my academic mentor, I dropped all math classes and changed my degree plan from Engineering *(what was I thinking?)* to Elementary Ed.

Ariana, emerging from the dressing room and strutting toward me as if on the catwalk, asked, "What do you think?" The gown was sleeveless with a V-neck that plunged to a still-respectable but intriguing depth. The silk fabric draped softly around her torso and swayed gently at her toes. She stopped, twirled so her back was to me, then glanced over her shoulder. Soft waves of black hair fell down the middle of her back, luxurious against the dark green cloth.

"You better give yourself an extra thirty minutes to get dressed," I said.

She looked back at me, her brows furrowed. "Why?"

"Because after seeing you in that dress, Dawson is going to need to detour through the bedroom."

"As if he needs an excuse."

Oh, oh. Trouble in paradise.

~~~
~~~

Our next stop was for shoes. There is only one store in Ariana's mind when it comes to shoes, so we left a deliciously cool mall, trekked across a steaming hot parking lot, climbed in a sauna-like vehicle, and zipped down Loop 360. The air conditioning had nearly cooled the SUV to tolerable when we arrived at The Village at Westlake, a high-class strip mall catering to the financially gifted.

I opened the door letting in a blast of mid-August heat. "Sonovagun!" I exclaimed, slamming the door. "You'd think by six o'clock it would cool off a little. I'll just wait here with the motor running and the AC on."

"Oh, quit griping and move your butt," Ariana said, opening the back door and removing her new plastic-wrapped gown from the utility hook.

I grabbed my purse and grudgingly followed her across the egg-frying hot blacktop toward a store with large brass letters reading *ARIANA V.* above the door. The retail shoe store is one of three that Ariana owns. The others are located in facilities catering to the affluent of Dallas and Houston. In between modeling and carrying on lousy relationships with lousier men, Ariana had earned an MBA and used it. The "V" in Ariana V. stands for Villarreal—her maiden name.

"I have a copy of *The Joy of Sex,*" I said. "You want to borrow it?"

"Where do you come up with this stuff?" she asked, her voice rising an octave.

"Ariana. Don't be a prude. You and Dawson have been married five years. You have to have sex."

"I know. Too often," she grumbled.

I like Dawson Wu. Dawson is the musical director of the Dulcinea Symphony. He is second-generation Chinese American, twelve years Ariana's junior, a good eight inches shorter, and the exact opposite in temperament. He is passionate, like one would expect from a gifted composer-conductor and quick to anger but quick to forgive—unlike Ariana who is good at holding a grudge. It was Dawson's playful, passionate side that attracted her in the first place, but it looked like something had cooled the passion.

"Are you mad at him?" I asked.

"No. I'm not mad at him."

"Then why don't you want sex?"

"Shhhh," she hissed, glaring at me as she opened the carved wooden door.

"Ariana!" Joan, a petite woman in her sixties, lit up when she saw her boss. "What a nice surprise."

"Hi, Joan," Ariana said, transforming the icy glare she'd given me to a warm smile for her store manager. "How are you?"

After they exchanged hugs, Joan turned to welcome me with a handshake and smile, then turned back to Ariana. "What brings you to town?"

"Shopping. I need to find a pair of sandals to go with this dress." She held up the gown. "Do we need to discuss business first?"

"Did you get the reports I faxed this morning?"

"We left early. They're probably waiting in the fax tray at home," she said. "Is there a problem?"

"Not at all. I think you'll be pleased with the financial report."

Ariana had been unlucky in love, until Dawson, but overwhelmingly fortunate in business. I, on the other hand, had been blessed with a wonderful husband and, until recently, a less-than-lucrative income. I don't believe Ariana would have ever changed places with me, and the reverse applies. We are each content in our own lives. At least, Ariana *had been* content.

While the two shoe specialists scoured the racks for a match to the dress, I searched the ceiling for an air conditioning vent.

Locating one, I stationed myself beneath it then looked around admiring the store. Ariana V. is very modern—designed in light wood, glass, mirrors, and lots of empty space, which my friend pays an arm and a leg for, but since her patrons will pay two arms, two legs, a kidney and a month's wages for the shoes she carries, the overhead is justified.

The incredibly expensive Cole Haan alligator mules Ariana decided on would never have received the American Podiatric Medical Association's seal of approval, but to Ariana, style is more important than comfort, so she was quite pleased when we set off for home.

Home is Dulcinea, a small city of about 70,000 people, surrounded by farms, ranches, and petrochemical plants. I live in Dulcinea because it's where my husband grew up. Ariana lives there because I introduced her to her present husband, Dawson—the one that isn't getting any sex.

"I think you need to see your GYN," I said, watching long shadows fly past the window.

"Why? I had an exam last month."

"Did you talk to her about your problem?"

"I don't have a problem. Dawson's got the problem—too much testosterone."

"Maybe you don't have enough," I said. You know women our age...."

"I don't have a problem," she said, glaring again. "Let's talk about something else."

This was the same woman who spent a week in Hawaii on her honeymoon and never saw the ocean. *She had a problem.*

Chapter Three

Around ten-thirty, Ariana dropped me at the front door with my few packages. Thurman and I live in the same house we bought when the kids were small, on ten acres just outside the northern city limits. The red brick house has a small fenced-in yard surrounded by pasture. It's a two bedroom-two bath that grew into a three bedroom-three bath when Marissa turned eight and started demanding privacy from her little brother.

Except for the front porch light, the house was dark. I unlocked the front door, flipped on the living room lights, and walked straight back into the kitchen where I found part of our menagerie. The two cats think the table is their own royal dais. Agatha is a black tortoise-shell, very petite with short-hair. She is a huntress, very independent but occasionally she'll let us pet her. Agatha sheds like crazy. Melrose came from the same litter but is her complete opposite. He's happy to be attended to like a fat Roman emperor. A gray and white long hair who weighs in at twenty-three pounds and stretches out to nearly a yard long, Melrose sheds like crazy. I dropped my purse and package on the table next to them sending up a cloud of cat hair.

On the ride home, I'd swept away thoughts of Gary and Claire, replaced them with the Ariana-Dawson situation, then started thinking about my own marriage. I counted up how many nights Thurman and I had fallen asleep right after the ten o'clock news, and when I ran out of fingers and started on the toes, I decided I'd better do something about it.

I made a pit stop at the bathroom (it's a long ride from Austin) then went to the den. I searched the CDs, found what I was looking for, walked back through the kitchen and utility room, and slipped though the back door.

The backyard once seemed overly congested. When Marissa and Sam were small, it held a swing set, trampoline, and above-ground pool along with yard toys and various animal pens, cages, and houses. Now that the kids are grown and gone, sadly, it looks very large and neat.

Thurman's workshop is within shouting distance of the back gate, which I unlatched and slipped through into the pasture. Our cattle had bedded down nearby, and I could hear them chewing cud and making other bovine noises. We have ten cows, seven calves, one bull, and one very old horse. Blue must have seen me, because he lumbered my way. I patted him on the neck. "Sorry, Old Man. I didn't bring you anything to eat," I said, but he followed me to the workshop anyway.

The lights glowed through the windows, and Shania Twain's music leaked out through the less-than-airtight seals. I opened the door. Sawdust, our golden retriever, jumped up and danced around me begging for an ear-scratching. Thurman sat with his back to the door, undisturbed.

I reached down to turn the radio off then leaned back seductively against the doorjamb. Thurman looked over his shoulder. "Hi. You're back," he said, turning back to the piece of wood in his hand, oblivious to the siren at the door.

My husband is a woodcrafter, an artist. The table he was presently working on was an octagonal card table commissioned by a wealthy New York businessman who'd seen Thurman's work on his website. The pedestal, carved from a solid block of wood, depicted four clawing lions' paws. When finished, the top would be a depiction, in inlaid wood mosaic, of a pride of lions attacking a wildebeest.

I moved across the room to stand directly behind my husband, leaned down, and kissed him on the neck. "You going to finish soon?" I purred.

"About another hour."

"Are you sure?" I whispered.

"Am I her?" he asked. So far, the seduction scene I'd played out in my mind was not going according to plan. Thurman is hard of hearing due to the abuse his ears have taken from years of loud saws and other woodworking machines.

I moved around to the other ear. "Are you sure?"

"Sure, I'm sure," he said, still not catching on.

I tried another tactic—running my tongue along the hair line on the back of his neck. It tasted salty, and I had to pick some sawdust off my tongue, but it got a response. Thurman shivered.

"All right, now," he said, sounding aggravated. He continued to work.

I walked over to the stereo and pushed the button for the CD tray. There's nothing like a little sax to set the mood. I dropped a David Sanborn disc in the drive and turned the volume to just too loud for me which made it just right for Thurman. He put down the wood and turned toward me.

I reached up, unbuttoned my top button, and wiggled

my left eyebrow, tauntingly. He lowered his brows in a *what are you up to?* look. I winked, slowly licked my lips, and opened the next button. From my previous self-description—deficiency of height, over-allowance of fat cells, oh yeah, and frizzy, red hair—one might expect total disinterest on Thurman's part. However, I've got several features going for me. I have, I've been told, beautiful blue eyes, a cute nose, and boobs. We're not talking normal, everyday boobs here. These are the Dolly Parton, in-your-face variety. I don't have the rest of Dolly's curves, but I've definitely got the bazookas, and right then, I had them aimed directly at Thurman.

"Do you want to take a shower with me?" I asked, teasingly.

"Huh?"

I gave up trying to communicate by talking, finished unbuttoning my blouse, sauntered by, dropping the blouse on his head as I passed. I walked into the bathroom he'd put in a few years back to shut me up about his dragging woodshavings in the house, turned on the shower, adjusted the temperature, and started out the door, then came to a screeching halt. Thurman stood in the doorway in nothing but a grin.

Chapter Four

The next morning, I awoke sated and starving. I rolled over, wrapped my arms around Thurman, and kissed him. He returned the kiss and called me a sex maniac.

"Let's stay in bed this morning," he said, turning away from me to go back to sleep. Obviously, he, too, was sated.

"I'd love to," I said. "But we have a lot of work to do, so you may as well get up and get ready."

"Hhhmmm," he growled into his pillow. "I don't know how I let you con me into this."

"Because you love me." I smacked him on his bare behind and got out of bed. "I'll start breakfast while you're getting your shower."

~~~

I was spooning cooked scrambled egg, sausage, and cheese mixture into a bowl when Luis rapped on the kitchen window. I waved him into the house.

"Mornin', Miss," Luis said.

"Good morning, Luis. Set those on the table for me,
~~~

please," I said, pointing to a stack of plates. He picked up the plates without another word, set them on the table, and sat in his usual chair.

Luis Anzualda is twenty-four and as quiet as a paint brush soaking in turpentine. His dark brown eyes are framed with lashes that would take half a tube of mascara for me to acquire. He is one of my former students—one who didn't graduate.

Academically, Luis was in the bottom of his class. It's not that he was unable to learn. On the contrary, Luis is extremely bright. Too bright. He attended classes, he read the texts, and he spent hours in the library. Luis knew that he knew the material being presented. But he didn't care if the teachers knew he knew. He wouldn't hand in homework. He would not take tests. He would listen and read and draw, which is where his intelligence was revealed to me, in his art.

It was also revealed to Thurman, who was so impressed with Luis' ability that he offered him a job. That was all the excuse Luis needed to drop out (against my very loud protests). Luis has worked for us for six years. He had arrived early his first day of work and joined us for breakfast. It became one of the perks of the job. One Luis did not relinquish even after he married his darling wife, Monika, two years ago.

"Hey, Boss," Luis said.

"Hi, Luis," Thurman said, walking into the kitchen. He looked down at the stove top. "Mmmm. *Tacquitos.*" He opened the refrigerator, removed a jar of *picante* sauce, swatted me on the backside in retaliation as he passed, causing Luis to laugh, and made a racket in the silverware drawer before landing at the table.

"Did you get everything loaded to take to the community center?" he asked, handing Luis a fork.

"Most everything. Mrs. Soto wanted to keep one of the

backdrops until this morning. She wasn't finished with it."

I placed warmed flour tortillas on the table and sat down. "Weren't they finished painting?" I asked, alarmed.

"They finished. One of her students had been sick. He needed it to do his report."

"Whew. That's a relief," I said. "I was afraid with everything else, we were going to be slapping on paint at the last minute, too."

Luis and the students of Chapman High, the school where I'd been the librarian, had painted twelve by twenty foot canvases to be used as decorations for the benefit. The grandiose theme of the fund raiser was *European Rhapsody—An Evening of Fine Music, Fine Art, Fine Friends.* Olga Perez, the principal of Chapman, agreed to provide the workers if I would tie the project into the teachers' educational objectives, provide the materials, and allow the school to keep the backdrops after the benefit. Ariana rounded up free paint and canvas, Willi sweet-talked Luis into supervising the students, and I worked with the faculty on lesson plans and in the classrooms helping teachers and students with the various projects. (So much for retirement.)

"We'll have to pick up that canvas this morning," Thurman said, reaching for a tortilla.

"I can go by the school while you two get started hanging the other backdrops," I said.

"How are we going to know where to put them?"

"Ariana and Willi will be there. If I had you hang them, they'd come along and have you rearrange them, anyway." I glanced at the clock. "We're supposed to be at the community center by eight-thirty. Inhale those tacos!"

~~~

I made it to Chapman by eight thirty-five. The campus is Dulcinea Independent School District's attempt to battle the high dropout rate. A year-around campus located in a converted warehouse on the south side of town, Chapman
~~~

houses approximately 250 students. Classrooms are set up with no more than sixteen kids who work at their own pace on individualized lessons created by their teachers.

Most successful adults can recall a relative, friend, or teacher who was a major influence when they were growing up. The at-risk students can't. The teachers of Chapman High are mentor, parent, teacher, and counselor all rolled up in one. The students remain in the same class with the same teacher all day in order to make a stronger personal connection. For many of the kids, that connection is the only thing that keeps them from failing not only in school, but in life.

After visiting a few minutes with the school secretary, I wandered down the hall to Cindy Soto's room. Cindy is in her late twenties and pregnant with her second child. She's six months along, but still able to kneel (unlike me—and I don't have pregnancy as an excuse, just bad knees) next to a student's desk, which is where I found her, helping a boy with algebra.

I stood in the open doorway admiring a mural of Venice's Grand Canal which hung along the back wall. The painting was from the perspective of a gondolier with the rippling water of the canal before him and stuccoed buildings along the banks on either side. A student sitting at Cindy's desk next to the door looked up and said, "Hi, Mrs. Matheson."

"Hi, Leticia. What are you working on?"

"Government," she said dejectedly.

"Keep at it," I said, making a face. "It's one of those necessary evils."

Leticia stuck her tongue out at the question she was struggling with, shrugged with resignation, then went back to work.

Cindy rose to her feet. "Hi," she said. The student she'd been helping looked up. Cindy tapped his textbook to draw him back on task.

"It looks like a traditional classroom today. Boring old worksheets and textbooks," I said.

She looked around laughing. "I'm happy for a little peace and quiet, boring or not. You should have been here a little while ago. We were *in Italy*," she said pointing to the backdrop, "and Freddy serenaded us with his version of opera."

"That's an exciting way to start the morning," I said.

"You wanna hear?" a tall, skinny kid asked.

"Spare us," his teacher said. Freddy grinned and turned back to the computer terminal. "Actually, his presentation on the life of the Italian tenor, Enrico Caruso, was excellent."

"The presentations I saw last week were great. And the kids created some beautiful paintings," I said. "I am so pleased. They'll be a hit at the benefit."

"Can we go?" one of the students asked.

"Tickets start at one hundred dollars per person."

"Damn!" another one said.

"Julian!" Cindy admonished.

"Sorry, Miss."

"It's going to be mostly symphonic music and old fogeys, Julian, but I'll take pictures for you," I said.

"Deal!"

I turned back to Cindy. "Can we get some kids to load that for me?" I asked, indicating the canvas.

Nine kids piled out of their desks and surrounded us. Cindy quickly selected three and sent the unhappy others back to their seats.

As she and I stepped into the hall, I asked, "Is Valerie in school? I didn't see her in your room."

"She's out at the daycare center."

"I'll pop in and see her when we get loaded. Thanks again for all the hard work."

"Thank *you*. The kids learned a lot and had a great time

doing it."

After supervising the loading of the canvas and thanking my helpers, I walked to the portable building that served as the daycare center for teen parents. Those students attend mandatory parenting classes two hours per week, one of which is spent in the daycare center with their own children practicing skills taught in class.

I peeked in the door. A male student leaned over a crib, gently picked up a baby, and held it against his chest. As I entered, Althea Gilbert, the teacher in charge, waved at me. She sat in a rocking chair holding another infant. Althea, a former pediatrics nurse who had returned to college to earn a teaching certificate, had been a real find for the high school.

"Is Valerie here?" I asked.

"With the toddlers," she said pointing to the far end of the portable.

When I retired, the mentor coordinator asked if I would volunteer to take on a student. Since teachers never quit teaching, even when retired, Valerie Ybarra, who presently sat on a blue tumbling mat rolling a yellow ball to three little darlings, was comfortably ensconced as my mentee. The babies surrounding Val just happened to represent, in one blend or another, the three major ethnic groups of the school. Valerie's little boy, Cody, who is Hispanic, Jerome Steele's son, Keeshawn, who is African American and Hispanic, and a little red-headed white girl I didn't recognize.

"Hi," Valerie said exuberantly. "What are you doing here? Are we supposed to go to lunch today?"

"No. I came by to pick up the Venice backdrop in your class." As I lowered myself to the mat, Cody toddled over and climbed into my lap. I played patty cake with him while I talked. "How's school going?"

"Good. I finished my economics today. I got an eighty-six on the final," she said proudly.

"Terrific. That's better than I did when I was in high school." (I hated economics. I think I ended up with a D plus, but I wasn't going to share that information with Valerie.)

"I'm almost through with World History, and Mrs. Soto is going to start me on Biology next week."

"If you need help, let me know. By the way, are you going back to the main campus when you're all caught up?"

She wrinkled her nose. "I don't think so. I've been away too long. The people I thought were my friends don't talk to me anymore," she said, studying the ball. Then she looked up and smiled. "But that's all right, because I have Cody and Isaac."

"Yes, you do," I said, pulling Cody's pudgy little hand off the chain he was trying to wrench from my neck. I handed him a board book that was close by, then reached out to steady Keeshawn who had decided to join us. When the little red-haired girl tried to climb in my lap with the other two, a small skirmish broke out, so I set each one aside and stood up.

"Are you meeting Isaac at the community center after school?" I asked. Isaac Molina, a former student, is Valerie's boyfriend and Cody's father. He works as an electrician's helper for Carlos Zuniga who was taking care of the lighting and sound for the benefit.

"No, Ma'am," Valerie said. "Cody's already wanting to help Isaac when he works, but he's not much help. Besides, my mom wants me to come over."

"Oh, well," I smiled. "I was just going to put you to work anyway." I walked toward the door. "Call me next week, and we'll set a lunch date."

Her face lit up. "Pizza?"

I frowned. "You have pizza all the time. Let's get dressed up and go somewhere nice."

"You mean I got to wear a dress?"

I looked at her black t-shirt and blue jeans. "It might be nice for a change."

She rolled her eyes but smiled.

"See you, Althea," I called as I opened the door. She looked my way and waved. I returned the wave, then shut the door, careful not to smash any grubby little fingers.

Chapter Five

The Dulcinea Community Center and its grounds take up thirty-six acres on Zarzamora Street between Travis and Bowie—just a few miles from the high school. When I pulled into the parking lot, I noticed Ariana's Lexus parked under the portecochere. (She doesn't have as many cars as she has clothes, but she's working on it.) Several other vehicles, including Willi's Mercedes, were sprinkled around the parking lot, and Thurman's truck was backed up to the large overhead door on the west side of the building. I parked beside it.

The domed main area of the center holds fifteen hundred people, so it looks very large when it's empty. I had expected to find the circular room bare, but when I entered, the decorating committee was already in full-swing.

Willemina, looking as if she just stepped off the cover of a Talbot's Petites catalog, was dressed in electric blue capris, matching leather slingback flats, and a white sleeveless top. She'd recently begun wearing her hair in a natural shag with long ringlets framing her heart-shaped face. The new 'do made her look closer to fifty than sixty. She supervised a group of men, including her husband, who compliantly moved, positioned, and repositioned tables at her direction. Thurman's brother Ray, who was in charge of the food, pushed a two-tiered cart, heavily-laden with stainless steel catering trays, into the kitchen. Far across the room from where I stood, Thurman and Luis balanced on ladders erected on either side of the Madrid canvas attempting to wrestle it into place.

Rising to the top of the dome, in the center of the room, stood the Eiffel Tower. I started toward it when I heard a voice from above.

"Heeeey, Darby! Up here." Atop scaffolding abutting the top of the aluminum replica, Tarzan waved.

Tarzan's real name is Edgar R. Burroughs, hence the nickname. He swears the "R" stands for Rice, but rumor has it, it's Ralph. Tarzan is completely misnamed. By his appearance, he should be called Long John Silver or Cheetah. His lower face is hidden behind an unkempt beard, a patch covers the eye he lost in a welding accident years ago, wavy brown-rapidly-changing-to-grey hair sweeps his shoulders, and he has his (and several other men's) share of body hair.

"How do you like it?" he asked, indicating the tower.

"Very impressive," I said.

"Thanks," he said, as he began his descent. When he reached the floor, he walked to my side. "Let me show you. I laid out the sections so they could be bolted together when I got here." He gripped an upright on the tower. "The base is in four sections; the center is in two and the top is one."

Ariana approached, smiling. "It is going to be safe for the models to walk around and under, isn't it Tarzan?"

"Yes, Ma'am. I guarantee my work. I haven't lost a model yet," he said.

"Just how many models have you encountered in your years in the oil field?" she teased.

He grinned lecherously. "You might be surprised."

Dawson appeared behind Ariana, winked at me conspiratorially, and said to Tarzan, "I don't believe anyone but you refers to the women you pick up at the bars as *models*. Let's see ... do you know the title to this?" He began whistling the tune to *Don't the Girls All Get Prettier at Closing Time.*

Tarzan and I laughed, but Ariana glared at her husband, then turned and stomped away.

We stopped laughing and faced Dawson who wore a look of complete bewilderment.

"What's wrong with her?" he asked.

Tarzan tried to make a joke of it. "Looks like she don't like you picking on me."

"I guess not."

Any other day, Ariana would have joined Dawson and teased Tarzan unmercifully. But whatever problem she didn't want to discuss yesterday, was still bothering her. She had flipped the jovial switch to *OFF* for all three of us. Tarzan shimmied back up the scaffolding. I gave Ariana's husband a sympathetic pat on the arm, then went in search of Thurman, leaving Dawson alone in his cluelessness.

I surveyed the room and spied Thurman and Luis moving their ladders and equipment away from Madrid, which, it seemed, they'd finally conquered, to an area with a bare wall. I reached them as they bent over to unroll another canvas. Vienna unfurled across the floor. A life-sized Lippizaner stallion rearing on his hind legs took up the foreground, with Saint Michael's Square and the Imperial Palace in the background.

"Wow. Doesn't that look great?" I said.

Luis straightened, arching his back and twisting from side to side. "It looks ... heavy."

"Hi, hon," Thurman said, standing and reaching out to pull me close for a kiss.

"Yeck, you're all sweaty."

He grinned wickedly. "You weren't complaining last night."

Luis blushed.

I winked at Thurman. "You're embarrassing Luis. He puts us in the same category as his parents. And no one wants to imagine their parents having sex."

"Uggggh," Luis groaned and staggered away as if he were sick. "I'm going to get some sodas," he yelled back over his shoulder. "Act your age."

Thurman pulled me close. "You want to act your age?" he growled suggestively.

"Later," I said pushing him away. "Someone needs to help me get Venice out of the Suburban."

"You're no fun." He turned to shout, "Hey, Luis. Get somebody to help you carry in that last tarp."

Luis agreed with a wave in our direction, though he wouldn't turn around to face us.

"Well, if you won't let me get frisky right here in the middle of the community center, you can run to the hardware store for me."

I laughed. "You'll have to find another time to get us arrested for public indecency. For now, tell me what you need ... wait." I held up a hand. "You better write it down. I'll just hand the list to the clerk, and they can find everything for me." I dug a note pad and pen out of my purse and handed them to Thurman.

Thurman explained what he needed as he wrote. Finishing the list, he handed me the pad and pen. "Call me from the store before you leave, just in case something else comes up," he said as he bent over the tarp to resume work.

I heard light-hearted conversation coming from the stage where Ariana, Willi, Carlos, and Isaac had gathered. Scampering up the south-end stairs, I joined them in time to hear Ariana ask, "Do we have back-up in case we blow a fuse?"

Carlos laughed. "You don't have to worry, even though you have gone a bit overboard on the lighting for this party. I did the wiring on this building, so I know what it can handle. But if all of Dulcinea goes out, we have a back-up generator, because 'the show must go on.'"

I walked up beside Willemina and gave her a shoulder-hug hello just as her cell phone rang.

She smiled. "Hi, Darby. Excuse me just a minute," she said, unclipping the phone from her belt. The cell phone matched her pants. I wondered if the capris and phone came as a set while I half-listened to her end of the conversation. What I caught was "... You can't? Well, have you found someone? ... I heard from her this morning ... Yes, I understand...."

Willi snapped the phone closed, clipped it to her belt and looked at me with that beseeching yet menacing look I'd grown to know so well. "Darby, my dear friend. I swear, your timing is impeccable," she said.

"I know what that means, Willi. That means you're about to saddle me with more work."

"But, Darby. It's because you're so capable. The two ladies who were going to take care of the table coverings have both come up with emergencies and can't make it. I need someone to pick up the linens from the rental store, deliver them, and spread them on the tables. It won't take you any time at all."

"That's what you said about the backdrops, and I believe I spent all summer working on those, not to mention the time I put in on the Eiffel Tower." I noticed Ariana, Carlos, and Isaac grinning at us. They were probably relieved the table coverings hadn't landed in their laps.

Willi spun me around to look out over the center of the room. "Just look," she said, pointing to the tower.

"It looks fabulous. It would never have been built if you hadn't found the specs on the original."

"That's what librarians do," I said, knowing I was being fed a line but not caring. "And it was a concerted effort. Luis used his software to convert the specs to scale and then you strong-armed Tarzan into building it."

"I didn't strong-arm him," she said innocently. "I sweet-talked him."

"You strong-armed him," I said matter-of-factly. "He just enjoyed it."

I heard Isaac laughing behind us. I turned to him. "Have you noticed that about Mrs. Henry, Isaac?"

"Yes, Ma'am. Mrs. Henry's pretty good at getting you to do something that can't be done."

"What does she have you working on?"

"I think she and Mrs. Wu think Carlos and me are magicians."

"What he means," Carlos said, "is they want lighting that would confound General Electric."

Willi and Ariana looked at each other. "Do you think now is a good time to mention the strobe?" Ariana asked.

Willi gestured toward Carlos with a flick of her eyes. In unison, the Amazon warrior and, her co-conspirator in sacrifice, the Zulu High Priestess, moved to either side of him, each taking an arm. Isaac and I laughed as they led away the hapless electrician.

"I'm proud of you, Isaac," I said, turning to him.

A few years back, I'd had to get one of my *bookends* (one of two bouncer-sized boys who spent time in the library) to separate Isaac and another boy when a fight broke out. The fight was very short-lived as my *bookend* was built like *The Rock*, and Isaac and the other boy were scrawny, both just over five feet tall. The young man who stood before me in the blue electrician's uniform resembled that previous Isaac only in the physical sense. Learning a trade had given him self-assurance and a sense of purpose that was missing when he was in high school.

"Carlos tells me you're learning fast," I said. "That you're reliable and very responsible. That's fine praise coming from your employer."

He smiled at me, the pride evident. "I like Carlos. He's a good boss."

"I stopped at the school and saw Valerie and Cody before I got here. That boy is getting big."

"And smart, Miss. You oughta see him when I'm working on my car. He knows which tool is the screwdriver and which one is the wrench. I have to keep my tool box locked up cuz he likes 'em more than he likes his toys."

We heard Carlos call to Isaac. Isaac waved to his boss. "I got to go, Mrs. Matheson," he said, turning to go.

"Isaac," I said, frowning. "When are you going to marry the mother of your child?"

In answer, Isaac trotted away, grinning.

I'd been made the official gofer, so I quickly made the rounds to ask if I could pick up supplies for anyone else while I was out. As I headed for my truck, Ariana joined me.

"Do you need something from the store?" I asked.

"No." She pointed toward the entrance. "There's *la chica* from Fronds and Feathers with some of the outfits for tonight. I need to tell her where to put the clothes. Darby, I am so jazzed," she said excitedly. "Carlos is going to be able to do everything I want, lighting wise, for the style show tonight. If the models remember their cues, it will be the coolest show."

"You're in a pleasant mood."

"Of course, I am," she said, as if she'd not shot a freeze-ray at Dawson earlier.

"I swear you are going through the change," I whispered.

"I am *not*," she said, through clenched teeth.

"You go from hot to cold—"

"I'm not having hot flashes!"

"I didn't say you were. Your *moods* go from hot to cold."

"Only when it comes to Dawson," she admitted.

"Ah, ha! You *are* mad at him."

"Hush," she said out of the corner of her mouth. Then she shouted a congenial hello to the woman who was directing two porters guiding an overloaded dress rack.

As I passed, a pile of scarves, handbags, and other accessories that had been perched atop the rack, slid from it and landed on the floor in front of me. I bent to help one of the workers pick them up. As my hand closed around the tangle of items, my throat constricted. I swallowed to fight back the nausea.

Ariana must have seen the blood drain from my face when I stood up. "Ooooh, no!" she said. "Not *bug guts*, again!"

"Got any soda crackers?" I said weakly.

Chapter Six

The trip to the hardware store was only the first of many. When I returned with the gadgets Thurman asked for, I was sent off once again to Hobby Lobby for decorating supplies and easels for the silent auction committee, to Radio Shack for some strange connector for Carlos, to Central Baptist Church to borrow the remote headsets the church uses in its yearly Christmas Pageant (needed by Ariana and her crew in order to communicate during the style show), to pick up lunch for everyone, and finally to collect the table coverings.

It was when I was returning from the last run that I saw Valerie walking in the direction of the community center carrying Cody. I beeped the horn to get her attention then pulled along side her and stopped. Unrolling the passenger window, I said, "Want a ride?" (I didn't have a child safety seat with me, but it was only a couple of blocks to the center.)

When Val got in and turned to me, I could tell she'd

been crying. "What's wrong, Valerie?" I asked.

"I hate my mother."

That wasn't what I'd expected. School problems, a fight with Isaac, maybe, but "I hate my mother"?

"You don't mean that," I said. "What happened?"

She started crying. "I don't hate her. I just wish she believed me."

"About what?"

"About Tony."

"Who's Tony?"

"Her new boyfriend."

"What about him?" My mind raced ahead, and I didn't like what it came up with. "Did he hurt you? Valerie? Did he touch you?"

"No, Mrs. Matheson," she said, wiping her eyes. "It's just the way he looks at me. And what he says to me. I don't like it." She set Cody in the seat between us and fastened the seat belt around his tiny waist. "I tried to talk to my mom about it, but she says it's my fault. She says I lead him on." In between sobs, she said, "I ... don't ... even like being in the same room with him."

I could feel my adrenaline building thinking about this creep getting close to Valerie. And as for her mother, well, I'd keep those thoughts to myself. I handed Valerie some Kleenex and waited until she got it all out, then asked, "Have you talked to Isaac about this?"

Her eyes flew open wide. "Oh, no. I'm afraid he'd try to do something. It would just make things worse. I'll be all right."

I wasn't too sure about that, but I put the Suburban in gear and drove to the community center.

I parked then turned to Valerie. "You better stay away from your mother's house for now."

"You don't have to worry," she said sadly. "I won't be going back."

I grabbed an armload of tablecloths from the back of the Suburban and followed Valerie and Cody inside. A volunteer's eight-year-old hurried over to us pulling a wheeled backpack. "You wanna see what I got?" she asked Cody.

"What do you have, Amber?" I asked, dropping the load of linens on a table.

Squatting beside the bulging case, she unzipped it. "Look." Stuffed animals, books, and crayons spilled onto the floor. Cody made a dive for a small black bear. "You want to play with me?" she asked. Cody stuffed the bear under his arm, squatted beside Amber, and peered into the treasure trove.

"Amber, will you watch Cody for me while I help Mrs. Matheson?" Valerie asked.

"Sure."

Valerie gained a baby-sitter, so I gained an assistant.

~~~

Thurman, Luis, and Tarzan had finished with their primary jobs and were helping Carlos and Isaac secure mesh-strung twinkle lights to the ceiling. When the entire ceiling was covered, Carlos warned everyone from the stage microphone that the lights would go out for a moment while they tested, so Valerie hurried over to be with Cody and Amber. The overhead lights went out, and we were in momentary darkness. When I looked up, the ceiling became a star-filled night sky. The next thing I knew, Thurman was beside me. He took me in his arms and began humming the tune to *I Only Have Eyes For You.*

As he danced me around the tables, I said, "I think you're getting randier since you started growing hair in your ears."

He turned his head so I could peer into his right ear. "What's it look like in there?"

"Like a rabbit's nest."

"I'd like to do a little *nesting.*"

"See what I mean."
~~~

The overhead lights flickered on, and Carlos announced they would have to fix a few connections then turn the lights out once more, but he'd warn us ahead of time. Thurman nuzzled my neck, released me, and left to help with repairs.

I was shaking off the sensuous fever that had enveloped me with Thurman's nibbles when Claire appeared before me. Talk about a cold shower!

"Do you think that's appropriate behavior?" she asked, with an insincere smile. She was dressed in a white linen sundress. She looked me up and down, visually criticizing my blue jeans, sneakers, and oversized "I Gave Blood" t-shirt.

"I enjoyed it," I said. "I really don't care if it's appropriate or not."

"I'm just kidding." Her voice was syrupy sweet.

Sure, you are, I thought.

"Have you met my son Nathan?" She motioned to a boy of high-school age standing behind her. "Come here, Nathan."

Nathan reminded me of a greyhound pup. One who'd lost the race. He shook my hand but gazed at my feet.

"Hi, Nathan," I said. "Nice to meet you."

He looked up at me and smiled slightly. "Thank you," he said. "It's a pleasure to meet you, Ma'am."

"Nathan is leaving for college in a few weeks. He's been accepted at Harvard."

The smile left Nathan's face, but he said nothing.

"Harvard," I said. "That's quite an accomplishment. Congratulations."

"Thanks," he said, looking at the floor. "Mother do you mind if I go help Dad?" He motioned to where Gary was setting up photographic equipment in front of Buckingham Palace.

"Not at all, darling," she said.

"He doesn't seem to be too excited about Harvard," I said when he was out of ear-shot.

"He's modest," she said, looking past me.

I turned and saw Willemina and Ray together, probably discussing the menu. Claire excused herself and hurried off in their direction.

"*¡Bruja!* She never passes up an opportunity to rub elbows with the rich and famous," Ariana said, appearing beside me.

The rich and famous Ariana referred to was Ray. He owns three restaurants in town. But that's not what makes him rich and famous. Thurman and Ray both played football at Dulcinea High. Thurman was good, but his big brother was better. He played for the University of Texas, was drafted by the Denver Broncos, was traded to the Pittsburgh Steelers, then went to the Houston Oilers—when there were Oilers in Houston—and finally retired after two seasons with the Cowboys. At 6'5" and 268 pounds, Ray was a formidable offensive guard. At his present three hundred and fifty, he makes an even more formidable chef and restaurateur.

"Claire never seems to want to rub elbows with you, and you're rich and famous," I said.

"I'll break her elbow if she tries rubbing it against mine."

"Oh, yeah. You're tough." I scanned the room. "Where is Dawson? I haven't seen him since this morning."

"Probably with his girlfriend."

"What?" I gasped. I'm glad no one was taking pictures right then, because I knew I looked like a dope with my mouth hanging open.

Ariana said nothing. I started to ask again, when I heard Valerie behind me.

"Is there anything else I can do to help, Mrs. Matheson?"

"The centerpieces need to be placed on the tables. You can help with those, Valerie," Ariana said.

The dust from the bomb she dropped still swirled around my head. I was dying to discuss it, but when Ariana looked at me again, her expression said, *Later!*

I followed her and Val to the boxes containing supplies for the table decorations. We worked like a moving assembly line. After I set a large bevel-edged mirror tile in the center of each table, Valerie placed a pink globe-encased candle on it, then Ariana completed the simple yet elegant design by sprinkling silk rose petals around the base of the candle. About ten tables along, we heard pandemonium erupt across the room. Valerie looked up, dropped the box of candles, and bolted away toward the London setup. Ariana and I quickly followed.

When we reached the agitated group, Isaac handed a crying Cody to Val and turned to face Claire. "I ought to pop you for that."

"I told you it was an accident," she said.

"You pushed him. You better stay away from my son, or I'll beat the crap out of you, lady."

"How dare you," Claire said, stepping forward.

Carlos wedged himself between a belligerent Isaac and an indignant Claire. "Let's calm down, now," he said, facing Isaac and slowly backing him away from Claire.

"I was just trying to get his dirty little hands off my dress when he fell down," Claire said emphatically.

A smear of chocolate accented her formerly pristine white dress near the hem. Valerie had stepped away from the group and was wiping the evidence from her son's fingers. Amber, whose lips were lined with chocolate, tried to distract Cody by placing a toy rabbit in his clean hand.

"Bull," Isaac said, looking past Carlos. "You pushed him. I saw you."

"Tell them," Claire screeched at Gary.

Gary stumbled forward from where he'd tried to disappear through the gates of Buckingham Palace. "I ... she ...

It ... it was an accident."

She glared at Gary angrily as if he'd been the one at fault, then turned to address Carlos rather than Isaac. "See? I told you. It was an accident. That kid doesn't have any business being here anyway."

Ariana was right. Claire was a witch.

Isaac raised his fist. "If you touch him again, I'll kill you."

I quickly moved to Isaac's side. "Isaac," I said. "Cody seems to be all right. He isn't even crying anymore."

Isaac dropped his fist to his side, but his jaws were clenched, and the look he gave Claire spoke volumes. He turned and accompanied Carlos and me up the stairs to the stage.

He flopped down in a chair at the light board. "Why are you taking her side?" he asked angrily.

"I'm not taking her side, Isaac," Carlos said. "I saw what she did, but sometimes it's better to drop it."

"I'll drop her."

"You need to calm down. Now."

Isaac stood up violently. "You want me to quit, Carlos? I'll just quit."

The hot-headed kid in the library had reappeared. *If only I had one of my* bookends, I thought. But finesse rather than force was what was needed. I stepped in front of Isaac. "You don't want to quit," I said gently.

"How do you know?"

"Because you like Carlos, and I can tell how much you enjoy working with sound and electrical systems. You're naturally good at it. Besides," I said, "you want Cody to be proud of you, don't you?"

Isaac looked at me, then at Carlos, then at the floor. He sat down.

"This is the first job you've had that you really enjoy. Carlos is depending on you, and so am I."

He looked up at me.

"Okay, Mrs. Matheson. But I'm not going back out there. Carlos, I'm not going back out there until that ... until she's gone."

"That's all right, just settle down," Carlos said. "You've got plenty to do back here anyway." He patted Isaac on the shoulder then disappeared through the curtains.

"She should be leaving soon, but I'll take Valerie and Cody home if you want."

"Thanks," he said, turning back to stare at the switches.

I pushed my way through the curtain and saw Willemina walking Claire and Nathan to the door. From this distance it looked as if Willi was in fourth placating gear, fixing to shift into overdrive. She was handling Claire. Carlos and I had calmed Isaac. It seemed the worse was over. But had I known what was to come, I would have let Isaac quit.

Chapter Seven

After dropping Valerie and Cody off, I drove home leaving plenty of time to feed the animals and shower and change for the benefit—I thought.

When I reached the house, the gate leading into the pasture gaped open. Not a cow in sight. Blasted horse! Blue had lifted the wire closure with his nose again. He and the cattle were wandering the neighborhood.

Getting the cows back was easy. I tossed a bucket of feed into the trough, grabbed the police whistle off the hook in the barn, and blew. Five minutes later, bull, cows, and calves pushed and shoved to find a place at the trough.

The horse usually comes when the cows do, but Blue must have found something better to eat than what the whistle promised. I started down the lane. When I reached the Sherman place, I saw Allen, Alex and Aloysius wrestling in the front yard. Their mother insisted on sticking with Al after their oft-laid-off father. Why she couldn't use Alfred or Albert is beyond me. Little Aloysius will be a great fighter by the time he's grown. I heard fists connecting with ribs, grunts, "ow," "eat cow turds," "you boogerhead," "anus face," and a few more artistic expletives. The boys are nine, eight, and seven. If I had had three boys in rapid succession, I would have slit my wrists—especially if I'd given birth to those three.

"Boys. Watch your language," I said.

They stopped fighting long enough to look up, and like a chorus of angels, sang, "Hi, Mrs. Matheson."

"Have y'all seen Blue pass this way?" I asked, walking toward the fence. Luckily, I looked down in time to sidestep a fresh pile of horse manure. "Never mind. I'll follow the trail." I looked down the road then back at the hellions. "You boys stop fighting."

"Yes, Mrs. Matheson," the trio sang.

I continued down the road and within moments the thuds, grunts, and swearing resumed. I spied a large black rump in the distance. Drat. He'd broken into Mrs. Lyttle's garden again, and I'd forgotten to grab a rope. I jogged the rest of the distance, grabbed a handful of mane and led him away from the carrots he was deftly pulling out of the ground. "Come on, you big pest. I don't have time for this. And Mrs. Lyttle is going to be mad."

Too late. I heard the screen door bang shut on the front porch. "I'm going to shoot that horse one day." Mrs. Lyttle, eighty-three, four-foot-nine, and about ninety pounds, held a broom in her hand. It's the only weapon she'd ever use on Blue.

"I'll be happy to load the gun for you, Mrs. Lyttle," I said. I led the horse over to her porch. "I'm sorry about those carrots. I'll pay for the damage."

She waved her hand. "Don't you worry about that. I planted too many, anyway. But you can send Thurman down to fix that fence for me." She pointed to a gap Blue had obviously used to get into the garden.

"Will tomorrow be all right? We're leaving for town

just as soon as I can get home and get dressed."

"That'll be soon enough. Just keep that animal penned up 'til then, or I'm libel to call the glue factory." She'd be more likely to set a place at the table for him.

"Yes, Ma'am. We'll see you tomorrow."

I was another ten minutes getting home. Thurman's truck sat in the driveway. As soon as I led Blue into the pasture, slapped him on the rump, and secured the gate, I dashed into the house, leaving twenty-five minutes to feed the dog and cats, shower, change, switch purses, and do my hair and nails.

Thirty-four minutes later, I was ready. The gown I'd made was based on a red gown Laura Bush had worn at George W's first inauguration ball. Put it on a short, chunky, busty Art Garfunkel and you'll have an idea of how I looked.

My patient husband sat behind the wheel of the Suburban blowing the horn. I hurried outside. Left to my own devices to open the door, I then had to figure how to buckle up without smearing my wet nail polish. I wanted to reach for a Kleenex to wipe the sweat that was trickling between my boobs in a ticklish river, but in order to protect my nails, I pressed the dress into my chest with the heel of my hand.

Now I had a sweat stain on the front of the dress. I looked at my fingertips. Crap! Somewhere between the door, the seat belt, and the sweat, I had botched the job. I'd have to live with gloppy fingernails. The chicken manure smeared on the heel of my sensible Naturalizer pumps, I would wipe off later.

~~~

The benefit was black tie, and to Thurman that means any black tie. He claims we don't attend enough formal events to warrant his buying a tuxedo, and he refuses to rent a tux that some pimply-faced kid probably wore to the prom. But Thurman does look very handsome in his black suit,
~~~

and there would be other fashion hold-outs attending, so he wouldn't be alone. Before we entered the community center, I gave him one last roll—with a lint roller that I keep in the glove box to fight the daily battle of magnetic cat hair.

We entered a doorway decorated with fake ficus trees wrapped in twinkle lights. Overhead, vines of fushia bougainvillea dripped from the wall above the door. Thurman gave our name at the reception table, and we were handed programs.

Willemina and Richard stood in the greeting line with several other board members of the Performing Arts Council. Willemina looked stunning in a gold off-the-shoulder Vera Wang number. Gold and diamond dangle earrings glittered, and a matching necklace adorned her neck.

They say opposites attract, and that is certainly true in their case. Richard, at six foot seven, towers over his wife. Slim, clean shaven with close-cut hair, Richard is the third generation of doctors in his family starting with his grandfather, the son of a former slave who became a wealthy and well-respected rancher in the area. Richard's quiet manner both contrasts and complements Willi's gregarious nature.

I hugged Willemina, and said, "I wish I could get Thurman into a tux. Richard looks so handsome."

"Thanks. I wish I could get him to enjoy wearing one. After all the functions I've dragged him to over the years, he still fusses when he has to dress up," Willi said. "Did you remember your camera?" she asked, reminding me of another duty she'd saddled me with.

"I'll dig it out of my purse as soon as what's left of my polish dries."

"Try to get plenty of shots of the biggest contributors. They like seeing their pictures in the newsletters and on websites. It will help when we hit them up at the next benefit."

"We?" I said.

"I know. You told me. This is the last benefit you're helping with. Of course, that's what you said the last time."

"Hush," I said.

"I'll hush. You take the pictures."

I snapped a salute. "Will do." Hugging Richard, I said, "I feel for you."

As I was about to proceed down the line, I heard Thurman ask, "Do you have to stand here much longer?"

Richard bent and asked Willemina in his very bass voice, "Dear?"

"About ten more minutes," she said, addressing Thurman. "Then you two boys can go play."

Thurman read her lips then turned to Richard. "I'll bring you a beer."

A wide grin of gratitude spread across Richard's face. "Thanks."

When we came to the end of the receiving line, I followed Thurman past the Eiffel Tower to an uncrowded bar. A string quartet played in front of the Vienna backdrop of the rearing Arabian horse and Imperial Palace. Looking in my program I read, *Quartet for Strings in G minor, Op. 10 by Claude Debussy.*

Willemina had managed to talk the members of the string quartet, a woodwind quintet, and a guitarist into playing background music for the evening.

Thurman received his order from the bartender, handed me two glasses of white wine, then picked up two mugs of beer. When we walked back to find the Henrys, the greeting line was just disbanding.

"Here you go," Thurman said, handing Richard a mug.

Richard took the mug with a nod of thanks and turned to Willemina. "My darling wife, I paid my dues by assisting you this afternoon, by giving a generous donation to the Performing Arts Center, and by standing in this God-awful receiving line. I will reserve one dance for you. As for the rest of the evening, enjoy your socializing. I shall be at the craps table." He kissed Willi on the cheek, then turned to Thurman, "Let's get while the getting's good."

We watched our husbands make their way through the crowd to the gaming tables set up as the focal point of Monte Carlo. The backdrop, barely visible over the crowd which had traded real money for play money, depicted Monaco's Grand Casino.

I handed Willemina a glass of wine and raised mine in a toast. "At least we'll know where to find them," I said.

She touched her glass to mine and winked conspiratorially. "And as long as the casino is open, they won't be whining about going home."

Chapter Eight

Willemina and I stood at the entrance and looked around the room taking in the culmination of four months of meeting, planning, designing, collecting, painting, hauling, begging, and arm-twisting.

To our immediate left, Gary Nathe snapped away at a pair of guests standing in front of Buckingham Palace and next to a live model dressed as one of the Queen's Guards.

"I hope you're paying that boy something," I said.

"This is a charity event, my dear. The soldier is a drama student at the college. I told him standing at attention all night as if he were a real guard would be great role-play practice for him."

"You're good. Air conditioning be hanged, it's got to be sweltering in that uniform," I said. I searched the crowd milling about the fake flora representing St. James' Park. "I don't see Claire. Are we going to be honored with her absence tonight?"

"I'm afraid not. Look a little farther."

I looked past London and into Venice. Dressed in a sheer leopard print gown, Claire stood talking with a handful of other women.

"Oh, goody. I was afraid I was going to have a wonderful evening. By the way, thanks for getting rid of her this afternoon. What did you say to get her to leave?"

"I told her, if she didn't get her dress to the cleaners quickly, it would be ruined. She's sending the cleaning bill to Carlos."

"What? ... Why?"

"Cody wiped chocolate on her dress. Cody is Isaac's child. Isaac works for Carlos. She figures she'll have a better chance of getting restitution from Carlos than from 'that trouble-making, bound-to-dropout little bastard.' Her words. Not mine."

"Did you set her straight?"

"I told her Isaac had graduated from high school in May, that he was not a trouble-maker, and he was behaving as would any protective parent."

I was about to ask Willi if Ariana had spoken to her about Dawson, when the mayor and his wife joined us.

After a few minutes of visiting, Willemina again mentioned pictures. Unable to escape my last assignment, I unzipped my un-stylish but handy-for-carrying-everything-but-the-kitchen-sink purse, dug out my trusty ten-year-old Minolta, and snapped a few pictures of Willi with the Honorable and his missus.

Excusing myself, I started to make my way around the room. Gary was talking to the young couple whose picture he'd just taken, so I asked if I could take a picture of him pretending to take a picture of them. After that, I snapped one of the sweaty guard, then wandered over to Venice. Thankfully, Claire had moved on.

I took half a dozen pictures of patrons crowded around tables and in front of the backdrop. The woodwind quintet was milling about, not yet ready to begin playing, as the string quartet in Vienna had not yet finished their set. The members of the quintet were happy to pose for me, so I clicked away.

I went on to check out Monte Carlo. There was very little posing here. Most of the patrons were intent on gambling even though the chips could not be exchanged for money. They could be spent only at the live auction or silent auction—of course, real money would also be accepted—but at the end of the evening, if a patron had not used his chips at either auction, he would be holding worthless plastic discs. It was win-win for the benefit—not so for the gamblers. But it was all for a good cause.

I found Thurman standing next to the stickman at the craps table. Richard stood at one end. I snapped his picture as he leaned in, tossed some chips on the table, and called "hard eight." I snapped another of Thurman giving Richard a high-five after the hard eight hit.

Dawson sat at a blackjack table nearby. He wore a double-breasted tuxedo with satin lapels. His straight, black hair is cut in a short shag. When he conducts, his hair bobs and weaves in a wild dance of its own. At the gaming table, it was sitting one out.

I walked up to him. "How's your luck?"

He swiveled around. "Hi, Darby." He turned back to the dealer, made a motion for another hit, then held. "So far, I'm even," he said.

"That's better than losing," I said. "Where's Ariana?"

"Probably backstage getting the models ready." He glanced at his watch. "The style show starts in about an hour." He turned over his cards, watched as the dealer raked away his bet, then put up another ante. He turned to me again. "I'll be glad when this soirée is over. Ariana has been a.... *You* know how she's been acting. This benefit is putting a strain on our marriage."

I didn't want to tell him it wasn't the benefit, but until I knew exactly why Ariana had said "with his girlfriend" I figured I better just keep quiet.

I stood behind Dawson for a few minutes pretending to watch him play cards. What I was really doing was trying to get any little vibe that confirmed or denied Ariana's suspicions. Nothing. There was *nothing*. Not getting *bug guts* could mean nothing was going on. It could also mean I couldn't pick up on the *something* if anything illicit *was* going on ... probably because I didn't want it to be true. I wished Dawson good luck and moved on.

Between Monte Carlo and Vienna was the door leading into the rodeo arena. When the committee was planning the layout of the party, we discussed putting London by that exit and setting up an English pub just outside for cigar smoking, brandy, and darts, but in the end we chose elegance over charm. Since the community center is a non-smoking facility, the smokers in the group had to go out front to smoke and sweat under the covered walkway.

I walked through Vienna, taking pictures of the guests and the string quartet, which was now playing Strauss. Another door between Vienna and the stage, which was part of the Paris display, led into the kitchen. Waitstaff walked out carrying trays of savory meats, shrimp, vegetables, pastas, and pastries. I walked into the kitchen where I snapped a photo of Ray, who resembled a clean-shaven Paul Prudhomme, swirling a pan of tortellini in Alfredo sauce over the gas stove. I thanked him for donating the food and waitstaff to the benefit. "When do you get to stop working and start partying?" I asked.

"We're closing up the kitchen when the style show starts. I wouldn't want to miss that."

"I hate to disappoint you, Ray. Ariana's not modeling. She's directing."

"Oh, shoot," he said, snapping his fingers. Then he grinned. "Oohh, but there will be other foxy ladies strutting the cat walk."

"Down, boy. You're married."

"I'm not dead."

"You're going to be if Debbie catches you," I said, though I knew Ray had been caught several times in the past by his long-suffering wife. Debbie's put up with more than most wives should have to, but she's a good Catholic, so no matter what Ray does, Debbie forgives him.

"Debbie doesn't have to know," he said.

"Later, Ray."

I climbed the stairs to the stage, went behind the curtain, and searched backstage for Ariana, whom I found in a tightly packed room of high school and college-aged girls applying makeup, styling hair, and getting dressed in the latest fashions from the finest wholesale and retail clothing suppliers in the area: Fronds and Feathers, Simon's, Double D Ranch Wear, and a half-dozen other stores. Ariana had even talked a designer friend into loaning some menswear from his collection for the male models who were housed in another dressing room.

Ariana stopped bossing long enough to talk. "See. It's going to be just fine," she said.

"Good," I said, unsure if she meant the show, the benefit, her marriage, or something that completely escaped me.

"The *bug guts,*" she said. "It's over. Willemina smoothed everything out. You were right. It was about Claire. Claire and Isaac. But it's over. It is, isn't it?"

I shrugged. "I haven't had any *bug guts* tonight, but I've been busy, and it's noisy, and I really don't want to think about Claire—so, I guess my answer is—I hope so."

"If you're not going to put my worries to rest, go away."

"OK. But first, tell me about Dawson."

"Not now. I don't have time to talk about it, and I don't

want to think about *ese pinche cabron."*

"There's no reason to call him names." I wasn't exactly sure what a *pinche cabron* was, but I knew it wasn't nice.

"Yes, there is," she said.

There was a loud knock on the door behind me. I opened it and peered out. It was Isaac.

"Hi, Mrs. Matheson. Can I come in?" he asked, innocently, while trying to see past me into the room of half-dressed girls.

"Nooo. I think I'll come out."

When I'd squeezed out and closed the door behind me, I asked what he needed.

"Here are the headsets for Mrs. Wu. Tell her they're working, but we should probably test them while she and her helpers are wearing them to make sure they won't have a problem when the show starts."

I took the three headsets, thanked him, and squeezed back inside.

"Here," I said, handing them to Ariana. "Isaac wants you to test them before the show."

"Fantastic." She took them and called across the room to her assistants. "I'll talk to you later," she said as she hurried away.

I wasn't going to find out why Ariana's husband had gone from the man "I can't live without" to a *"pinche cabron"* in just a few days, so I made my way back to the party. From the stage, I took some pictures of the Eiffel Tower and the far-wall which included Monte Carlo, Vienna, and London. Then I changed the lens to a zoom and snapped off some more. I'd brought eight rolls of twenty-four exposures and had gone through two. I changed the lens back to the 50 millimeter and walked off the stage to get pictures of Madrid's backdrop and the covered handcarts which held the silent auction items. The guitarist held his guitar as if he were about to begin playing, so I snapped his photo.

I spent some time visiting with friends, sipping wine, and watching Thurman lose at the dice table. When he'd lost enough, we strolled over to load our plates with yummies, then sat at a table and stuffed ourselves. We finished just as the overhead lights flickered off and on and an announcement was made that the casino and kitchen were closing during the style show, which would start in five minutes. The patrons made their way to tables and chairs set up along the stage and runway.

We had been entertained by the classics all evening, but Ariana had something completely different in mind for the style show. The lights went out. The curtains opened to the musicians who had reassembled on stage as a kind of mini-chamber orchestra.

Ariana's models paraded on stage, down the stairs, and around the tower to the compositions of Hayward, Lennon and McCartney, Sting, Jagger and Richards, and Clapton and Gordon. They started with a slow stroll to *Nights in White Satin* and *Fields of Gold,* picked up the pace with *Abbey Lane,* and at the end, broke loose like a clan of druids celebrating the full moon at Stonehenge to the final number, *Brown Sugar*—all of which was accompanied by strobe lights, spot lights, and fog machines.

When the last note faded and all the participants returned to the stage, the audience gave them rousing applause along with whistles and shouts of "encore," so Ariana led the procession of models as they sashayed one last time while the musicians played *Layla.*

The overhead twinkle lights came back on, sending the patrons back to the food tables, to the bars, and to look over the auction items. Thurman made his way back to the casino, and I headed off in the opposite direction to take more snapshots.

Tarzan, his hair pulled into a ponytail tied with a black satin ribbon, sat at a table in Madrid. Flanked by four coeds, the lovable Lothario yelled, "Get a picture of us," as he reached out with both arms to draw in the two nearest females. The other girls moved their chairs closer together, and I took a couple of pictures. "I want five copies of that, Darby. One for me and one for each of my ladies," he said.

He introduced me to his harem and asked me to join them. My first thought was to decline; but I changed my mind because my feet were killing me, and I was tired from lugging around my camera and overloaded purse.

I pulled out a chair and sat beside a little blonde who looked like a seventeen-year-old airhead. I try to not prejudge people, but it's pretty hard when it comes to Tarzan's companions since his tastes usually run to beauty and no brains. Nevertheless, I should have followed my own rule when it came to the blonde. She was twenty-six and an elementary school teacher working on her doctorate. The brunette with the waist-length hair did fit Tarzan's dating criteria. She asked if she could use my camera, and after several long minutes of instruction, finally understood that I had it set so she could just point and shoot.

Figuring that since the camera had survived my abuse for years, it could handle a few minutes with a ditz, I let the girl traipse off to take pictures of her boyfriend who had modeled earlier.

As the guitarist played selections of de Falla, I chatted with Tarzan and the remaining girls: one of whom was a receptionist, another—a makeup specialist at a local department store, and the teacher. With two educators at the table, the conversation revolved around school politics, curriculum, teachers, and kids. I was on my soap box about the ineffectiveness of state mandated testing when I was hit by an overwhelming urge to run, not walk, but *run* to the kitchen.

Chapter Nine

I excused myself, jumped up from the table, dashed through the crowd, and slammed through the swinging door coming to a screeching halt just inside. The kitchen staff stopped what they were doing to look at me. One worker held a stainless steel serving pan over the large double sink, another paused in wiping down the stove, and another hesitated before putting a coffee packet in the industrial-sized coffee maker.

I turned around when I heard the door swing open behind me, and Ray ask, "What the heck's going on, Darby? You tore in here like a wide receiver on a fourth down."

I looked around the room. Everything seemed fine. I turned to Ray and said sheepishly, "I thought I smelled smoke."

Ray and the other workers sniffed the air. "Nope. No smoke," Ray said. He told them to return to their tasks, then put his arm around my shoulders and turned me toward the door, saying, "Come on, I'll buy you a drink."

"Thanks, Ray. It's an open bar."

He had his hand on the door when a loud pop sounded behind us and shouts erupted from the workers. We turned to see flames shooting from the coffee maker. Ray dashed across the room, grabbed a fire extinguisher, and fired a geyser of white powder over the machine, counter, and wall.

The fire was soon smothered, but the noxious fumes, along with all the shouting, had drawn a crowd of onlookers, including Thurman. "What happened? Is everything all right?" he asked.

"Must have been a short," Ray said. He turned and spoke to one of the workers. "Open up those back doors before we have the fire marshal canceling this shindig."

"What are you doing in here?" Thurman asked me.

Ray answered. "She came in to tell me she smelled smoke." He squinted at me in consternation. "But that was before the fire."

"Just a coincidence," Thurman said, grabbing my hand and hustling me out of the kitchen and across to the nearest bar. He ordered us both a drink, then led me to an unoccupied corner to keep from being overheard. "You smelled smoke *before* the fire?"

"Of course not. Something told me to go to the kitchen. I made up the stuff about smelling smoke when Ray asked me why I had run in there."

"You're spooky."

"And you are losing all of our money gambling."

"No, I'm not." He dug into his pocket, pulling out a handful of high dollar chips. "I'm ahead."

"I'm happy to hear that. But what are you going to do with all that play money?"

~~~

What he did was pool his money with Ray, Dawson, and Richard. At the live auction, they bid on a deep-sea fishing trip out of Corpus Christi, which, to shouts of jubilation
~~~

and an end-zone dance by Ray, they won.

A little after midnight, Willi, Ariana, and I sat with our husbands at Tarzan's table. The rest of his groupies had left but the makeup specialist remained. She had dragged Ariana and Richard into a discussion about skin-care. I was deciding on whether to get up and go home or just crawl up on the table and sleep there when Gary walked up to Tarzan.

"Have you seen Claire?" he asked.

"Hey, Gare. Have a seat," Tarzan said.

"No, thanks. I'm packed up and ready to go, but I can't find my wife." He looked around the table. "Has anyone seen her?"

I got a really yucky feeling. One I tried to ignore. I hadn't seen her since the beginning of the evening.

There were a lot of heads shaking at the table. Some had remembered seeing her, but not recently.

"If you see her, tell her I'm looking for her."

We watched him walk away.

When he was out of earshot, Ariana said. "She's probably mad at Gary for not being Bill Gates and is somewhere pouting. Or maybe she went home with Bill Gates."

"Bill Gates wasn't here," Thurman said.

Willemina yawned. "Maybe we should have invited him."

"That's a good idea," Ariana said. "Next benefit, let's put him on the list. While we're at it, let's add Rupert Murdoch and Oprah."

"And don't forget Sam Walton's heirs," Tarzan said.

"Would y'all knock it off? Gary really is concerned," I said. I pushed up from the table. "I'll look in the ladies' room. Thurman, will you and Richard go look outside?"

The others stood and began the search. Ray went to the kitchen, Dawson and Tarzan and his friend went backstage, and Ariana and Willemina walked in opposite directions through each "city" asking the remaining guests if they'd seen Claire. I went into the ladies' restroom to look, then I ran a man out of the men's room and checked in there.

Unsuccessful, I returned to find that Ariana and Willi had turned the house lights on and were searching the room from the stage. I joined them.

"Any luck?"

They shook their heads. Then Ariana said, "You know what these decorations remind me of?"

"Europe?" I said.

"Las Vegas."

"Ariana," Willi said, "Remember the theme of the evening? European Rhapsody?"

"I know. But look." She pointed around the room. "The Paris Casino, The Monte Carlo, The Venetian."

I pointed to the backdrop of Buckingham Palace. "And what casino is that? The Excalibur? And what about Madrid? There's no Madrid in Las Vegas."

"Look, missy," she said, jutting out a hip. Don't be *una sabelotoda!* I said, 'It *reminds* me of Las Vegas.'"

"I'm not being a smart aleck," I said, doing my own little prissy wiggle that morphed into a shiver when a cold chill ran down my back. I choked out, "They ... found her."

"What?" Willemina stared at me.

"I mean—let's go see if Thurman and Richard found Claire."

Ariana grabbed my elbow and led me down the stairs a few steps ahead of Willemina. "They found her?"

"Yes. And it's not good."

"What are you two whispering about?" Willi asked suspiciously.

I slowed so she could catch up. "Ariana's calling me bad names in Spanish, because I was giving her a hard time about Las Vegas. Tell her to get her nails out of my arm."

"Look," Willi said, pointing to the door leading to the arena. Thurman had entered and walked directly to Gary, said something that seemed to alarm him, then led him out through the same door.

Ariana released my arm, and we hurried down the stairs. Thurman stopped us almost as soon as we entered the arena, quickly ushering us back into the main ballroom—but not before we saw Richard and Gary crouch beside the motionless body of Claire Nathe.

Chapter Ten

Claire was dead. Moments earlier, most of our party, myself included, felt exhausted and wanted nothing more than to go home, crawl into bed, and go to sleep. But death has a way of changing one's body chemistry. I'm not referring to the deceased's body chemistry, that's a given. I'm talking about the rest of us. Even if it is the death of someone you're not all that fond of, because of adrenaline, you can pretty well run on automatic whether you're tired or not. It was fortunate our bodies reacted this way, because we spent the rest of the evening, or rather, the wee hours of the morning, with the police.

When Thurman and Richard happened upon Claire's body, Richard did his doctor thing and realized it was way too late for medical treatment, so he stayed with the body and used his cell phone to call the police while Thurman found Gary to break the bad news.

It wasn't long before five patrol officers, two supervisors, three investigators, and the crime scene unit were swarming all over the place. The remaining guests were questioned. The police asked first for our names and contact information. When they were satisfied there was nothing more we could tell them, we were allowed to leave. It was nearly three-thirty in the morning when Thurman and I finally crawled into bed.

~~~

The phone rang at seven twenty-eight. At least, that's what I think the clock read.

"Mrs. Matheson? I don't know what to do," a panicked voice said.

"Valerie? Is that you?"

"The police took Isaac. What do I do?"

I could make out the sound of cars passing in the background along with a crying child.

I sat up in bed. "What are you talking about? Where are you?"

"I'm at the convenience store near my house. The police arrested Isaac," her voice broke into racking sobs.

"Calm down, Valerie. Tell me what happened."

Thurman rolled over and looked at me through sleepy eyes.

Somehow, through Valerie's sobs, Cody's wails, and the traffic noise, I learned the police had come to their house to ask Isaac questions about his argument with Claire—an event I had conveniently forgotten during my questioning but which another witness must have disclosed to the police. Being the act-first-think-later kid that he was, Isaac went from guarded to angry to shoving an officer, and now he was in jail.

"Oh, boy," I said, dragging myself out of bed. "I'll see what I can do, but I can't promise anything."

"Thank you, Mrs. Matheson."

"Don't thank me yet. Go home. I'll come over when I finish at the police station." I sighed and hung up.
~~~

"Don't spend any money bailing him out," Thurman said, rolling away and burying himself in the pillow.

My husband and I had had many a loud discussion over "Darby's Save the Children Fund" as he had referred to my tendency to put most of my teaching salary back into the classroom, library, and students. "Do you want to know what's happened?" I asked.

"No. It just better not cost us anything." He was snoring before I reached the bathroom door.

~~~

I stood at the reception window looking over the counter into a large office area. Four desks were arranged so the clerk or officer faced the counter. File cabinets lined the left side of the room. A large painting of four police officers with the American flag waving in the background hung from the opposite wall. A hallway ran the length of the back of the room.

A woman dressed in uniform rose from her desk, smiling as she approached. "Yes, Ma'am?"

"I understand Isaac Molina was brought in a little while ago. May I talk to him?"

"Are you a family member?"

"No. I'm Darby Matheson. I'm his teacher."

"I'm sorry. He can't have visitors."

"May I talk to the Chief?" Police Chief Jim Swanson is one of Thurman's fishing buddies.

"Would you mind waiting?" She pointed to some chairs lining the wall behind me. I took a seat.

A few officers walked in and out, but it was mostly quiet. I was alone in the waiting room for about five minutes when I was instructed to approach a locked steel door on my right. When I did, it clicked open. I stepped through and waited as it closed behind me. The same female officer came around the corner. She led me to an open door on the right, motioned me inside, then turned and left.
~~~

"Darby, come on in," Jim said, rolling his chair back from the desk and standing to shake my hand. "Want some coffee? I just made a pot."

"Thanks. Cream, please," I said.

While he walked over to a cabinet where a Mr. Coffee held a full carafe, I settled into one of the two upholstered chairs in front of his desk.

"How are things at Chapman High?" he asked.

"Didn't Thurman tell you? I'm retired."

"I wish I could retire."

"I could have put in another five years, but Thurman's business is doing well, and it was hire a bookkeeper or me. Besides, I got fed up with the politics."

He walked back, handing me one of two mugs he carried. "You haven't seen politics 'til you've worked in city government," he said.

"I bet."

Jim sat behind his desk. "What can I do for you?"

"I'm here about Isaac."

"Molina?"

I nodded.

"You can't see him."

"Jim, Isaac doesn't have anyone except his girlfriend and son. He's an orphan."

"That's too bad. But you won't be seeing him until Monday at the earliest. What connection do you have to Molina?"

"He was my student a few years ago. I'm his girlfriend's mentor. He's not a bad kid, Chief. He has a temper, but he reacts defensively. He doesn't always think before he acts."

"Did he think before he killed Claire Nathe?"

I flinched. "I thought he was being held for assaulting an officer."

"He was. But in the meantime, we found his fingerprints on the belt used to strangle her."

"Oh, my." I was shocked into silence. Then I remembered how Isaac had been dressed. His red boxers peeked out from above the waistband of his droopy jeans. "He wasn't wearing a belt."

"I didn't say it was his belt," Jim said. " He used one of the belts brought in for the show."

The accessories that I'd touched which gave me *bug guts.* "I'll bet my fingerprints are on there, too," I said automatically, then realized I'd just implicated myself.

"Oh?"

"Well, yes. I handled some of the clothing yesterday afternoon."

He nodded. "There are a few prints we haven't identified yet. Since you're here, let's get you printed." He stood up.

I remained seated. "Am I a suspect?"

"Everyone is a suspect. But you're an unlikely one. Do you have any objections?"

"No," I said, feeling nervous even knowing I wasn't guilty.

I followed Jim out of his office and down the hall. He introduced me to a female officer then asked her to fingerprint me. The fingerprinting machine seemed to be a cross between a computer and a copier. Because my hands were dry, she had me rub a little lotion on my fingertips then took my prints. First she asked for my right hand, taking each finger individually and rolling it from one side to the other across a glass plate. Then she took my index to little finger as a group. She did this for both hands.

"You might want to fingerprint the models and the others helping with the style show," I said to Jim.

"I've got two officers working on that now."

"It could be anybody, even me. But it's not me," I said adamantly. "And it's not Isaac. You can let Isaac go."

He shook his head. "We're not letting Isaac go. We have enough to hold him on the murder, and even if we didn't, he's still going to have to answer to resisting arrest and assaulting a police officer."

"May I please talk to him?"

"You can bail him out on Monday," the chief said.

"How much will that be?"

"Bond will be set at around $250,000. He'll have to come up with about twenty-five thousand."

"Twenty-five thousand?" Yikes! Isaac didn't have that kind of money. And Thurman had already made his feelings very clear. "What's the alternative," I asked.

"He stays in jail."

~~~

Willemina and Richard live in a beige brick, two-story house of about 5,000 square feet in the neighborhood known as Country Club. While there are three country clubs in Dulcinea, this area is *the* country club since it is the original, the most restrictive, and its members the most influential in Dulcinea.

Willemina and Richard met in Houston where Willi was majoring in Art History at Rice and Richard was at Baylor College of Medicine. In the early years of their marriage, Willi worked as a museum curator while Richard finished his education and residency.

Willi's house is a museum in itself. The kitchen is the Greco-Roman Room. The floor and cabinets are a natural oak, the counter tops black marble. Pottery in shades of browns, greys, and black depicting Atlas holding up the heavens, Romulus and Remus suckling the she-wolf, Apollo attempting to capture Daphne before she turned into a tree, and others adorn the space above the upper cabinets.

I sat at Willi's breakfast table looking out over the patio, the pool, the azalea-lined wrought iron fence, and onto the 17th green where a man wearing University of Texas orange shorts just missed a three-foot putt.

It was obvious from the aroma wafting out of the oven
~~~

that Willi had been up for a while concocting one of her fabulous breakfast pastries. She wore a pink robe and slippers, her hair was pulled back in a clip, and she wore no makeup. Even with little sleep, she was still drop-dead gorgeous. In the same condition, I'm Dracula's ugly sister.

Willi handed me a cup of coffee and sat down. "Do you think he did it?" she asked.

"Isaac has a temper, but I don't think he would kill anyone."

"I don't either," she said.

"I wish I'd been able to speak with him."

We heard the front door open then the click-click of footsteps coming toward us while another set of smaller, faster clicks and shuffles ran down the hall then back just as quickly. A moment later, Willi's oldest daughter Roslyn and her little girl came around the corner.

"Grandma!" Maya yelled, diving into Willi's lap.

Willi rocked her granddaughter back and forth in a tight hug.

"Good morning, Mother," Roslyn said. "Maya. Don't shout. Grandpa and Aunt Raven are probably still sleeping."

Willi nodded her head, kissed Maya on the forehead, then pressed her finger to lips. "Shhhh."

Roslyn turned to me. "Hello, Darby. You're here early."

"So are you," her mama said.

"We were going to sneak in and out without waking you. Maya left the little white purse you gave her in the playroom, and she thinks she has to have it." She looked at me and explained. "We're attending an out-of-town wedding."

"See my new shoes," Maya said. A blue sash belted her white lace dress. A matching blue bow tied back Maya's hair in a pony tail that cascaded in a tumble of black corkscrews. White patent leather shoes adorned her little feet. The white purse was clutched in her hands.

"You two look like you could use more sleep," Roslyn said.

Willemina said, "You're right about that. We had a late night last night. Claire Nathe was k-i-l-l-e-d."

"I can spell," Maya said. "M-a-y-a spells Maya."

"Very good, baby," Willi said.

"At the benefit?" Roslyn asked unbelieving.

"Um-hum," Willi said.

"Claire Nathe. That name sounds familiar."

"Claire owns ... owned an interior decorating business. Her husband owns Nathe Photography."

"Oh, yes. We used to get portraits done there. What happened?"

"She turned up missing after the benefit, and her b-o-d-y was found in the livestock arena," I said joining in the s-p-e-l-l-i-n-g for the benefit of the child.

"B-a-b-y spells baby," Maya said.

"Right. And what does r-e-s-p-e-c-t spell?" Willi asked.

"Aretha!" Maya said, jumping off of her grandma's lap. She danced around the table while singing "r-e-p-c-t shake it to me, shake it to me."

Willi and I laughed. Roslyn rolled her eyes. "Thank you, Mother. Thank you for winding her up for the long trip to Navasota."

We laughed even harder.

The oven timer buzzed, and Willemina rose from the table. She took an oven-mitt from a nearby drawer and removed a tray of mouth-watering peach buns from the oven.

"Can I have one, Grandma?" Maya asked.

"Sure you can, baby."

"Mom, will you wrap one up for her for later? We just had breakfast. Besides, I don't want Maya getting sticky glaze all over her dress."

Willemina wrapped three buns in foil, then wrapped the foil pack in a dish towel and handed it to Roslyn.

"Thanks. I'd stick around to find out about last night, but Curtis is waiting in the car," Roslyn said, taking her daughter's hand. "Come on, Maya. Dance your little behind out to Daddy. I'll call you later, Mother."

When she heard the front door open and close, Willi brought the remaining buns, plates, and forks to the table then refilled our coffee. "Roslyn has grown up to be such a sensible woman," she said, shaking her head. "And that man she married is just as dull." She grinned. "It's a good thing Maya inherited a few of my genes."

She returned the carafe to the coffee maker. Her smile faded as she sat down. "What are we going to do about Isaac?"

"I don't know yet," I said. "I guess the county will get him a court-appointed lawyer."

"We could have a benefit and raise some money, so he could hire a good one," she suggested.

"Haven't you had enough of benefits for a while?"

"I never get enough."

"I have a better idea," I said, resting my elbows on the table and leaning toward Willemina. "It doesn't make a bit of sense that Isaac killed Claire last night. I'd have an easier time believing he would have knocked the snot out of her after she pushed Cody yesterday than thinking he plotted to kill her hours later."

"So, what's your idea?"

I bit into a delicious peach bun, letting the peaches, brown sugar, and cinnamon caress my taste buds. "Mmmmm," I said.

"Your idea?"

"These are great."

"I'll give you the recipe."

"You think I want to bake them? I just want to eat them."

"I'll make you a dozen. What is your idea?"

"We find out who really killed Claire," I said, taking another bite.

Willemina used an exaggerated New Joisy accent. "Like nose around and find out who had it in *foir heh?*"

"You sound like a bad B-movie."

Her eyes sparkled. "It might be fun," she said. "Oh! We should give ourselves a name. All detective agencies have names."

"This is serious, Willemina. Isaac is in trouble."

"I am being serious. There's no reason we can't have a little fun while we are clearing Isaac of murder."

"OK. But you work on the name and a list of people we should contact who might know something about Claire Nathe. I'm going to check on Valerie."

I stood up. "Thanks for breakfast." I walked to the sink and set my mug and plate on the counter. "Call me later."

Chapter Eleven

Isaac, Valerie, and the baby live in a small, dilapidated frame house on the south side of town in a section called Pleasant Valley, a moniker eliciting the images of green rolling hills, flowers and butterflies, and children frolicking along a bubbling brook. *In your dreams.*

Pleasant Valley's major landmark is a graffiti-covered railroad trestle. Weed-filled lots and old houses, most of which are in need of major repair, if not demolition, line either side of pot-hole riddled streets. Most of the *Gun-free Zone* signs are punctuated with bullet holes, and drug-dealing and prostitution are the main businesses. The area should be renamed Destitution Dell.

I pulled into the yard and parked behind Isaac's old Chevy Impala lowrider. Even though it was broad daylight and all the bad elements were probably under their rocks waiting for nightfall, I was not comfortable getting out of my car. But since a sixteen-year-old girl and her eighteen-month-old baby were inside alone, I figured I'd better strap on my brass bra. I got out, tucked my purse tightly under my arm, locked the car, and ventured forth.

As I approached the house, I realized the wooden steps leading up to it were shot, so I would have to leap onto the porch. In *my* dreams. I looked first to my left then to my right then weakly called out, "Valerie?" Her face appeared in the ready-made peep hole—the missing top quarter-panel of the door partially covered with aluminum foil. Besides needing steps and a new door, the house was badly in need of a new roof, a paint job, and screens.

"Ms. Matheson." She unlocked the door and pulled it open. Why she bothered to lock it in the first place was beyond me. "Did you get him out?" she asked, her face filled with hope.

"No, honey. I'm afraid not."

Her face fell. "Oh." She stepped back. "You want to come in?"

I looked at the steps. "Is it safe?"

"If you stay on that side, you'll be all right."

I stepped gingerly up the dilapidated steps to the dilapidated porch and entered the dilapidated house.

"Do you want to sit down?" She gestured to the couch that had seen better days. It must have had legs at one time, but was now legless.

"Honey, if I sit down, you're going to need a crane to get me up." I felt a trickle of sweat run down my back and between my cheeks. I had an overwhelming urge to scratch, but I was supposed to be a good influence on Valerie, so I endured.

The baby wore only a disposable diaper. Valerie was in shorts and a sleeveless top. She, too, was perspiring. A fan sat in the window pushing hot air around the room. It was eleven o'clock. By two, the house would be an oven.

Despite its structural problems, Valerie had tried to pretty up the place. Though the stained carpet was worn right through to the bare wood in places, it looked as if it had been recently swept. A crucifix hung over the door. Pictures of the baby and the family were placed around the room. A playpen and stroller took up much of the living room area.

"I'm afraid I have some bad news."

The tears started up again when I told her Isaac was being held for the murder of Claire Nathe.

"He didn't do it."

"I know. But the police have enough evidence to charge him."

"But he didn't do it!" she wailed. I remained silent for a while as she spent some of the tear reserve. "What am I going to do?"

"We'll figure out something. In the meantime is there someone you can stay with?" I automatically thought of her mother then just as quickly dismissed that idea. "Your sister maybe? Your dad?"

She shook her head. "My sister lives with her husband's parents. My dad lives in Del Rio."

"Well, you can't stay here alone."

"We'll be all right."

I peered out the front window. I wouldn't spend the day in this neighborhood, let alone a night. "I wouldn't forgive myself if something happened to you or Cody. Besides, it's going to be a hundred degrees this afternoon. Get some clothes together and whatever you need for the baby. You can stay with us for a while."

"Are you sure?"

"Of course," I said, thinking Thurman might be put out for a little but only for not discussing it with him first.

I knew Valerie drove even though she did not have a driver's license, but I wasn't going to let her break the law while she was my guest, so I loaded the playpen and stroller in the Suburban while she gathered clothes for herself and the baby. "Do you have a car seat?" I asked, when she came down the steps.

She handed the baby to me, removed the car seat from Isaac's car, strapped it into mine, then strapped Cody into the car seat.

We stopped by a Speedy Stop for diapers, which I paid for over Valerie's objections, then headed for home.

Thurman wasn't in the house when we arrived, so I settled Valerie and the baby in the guest room then went outside to break the news.

I found Thurman replacing the wire used to keep the gate fastened—the one Blue removed regularly with his nose—with a heavy metal chain. "I'm back," I said, "but I'm not alone."

"Why am I not surprised?" he asked, looking up.

I went into my sales pitch. "If you could see where these kids live. In Pleasant Valley of all places. Ivan the Terrible wouldn't feel safe in that neighborhood. Valerie and the baby shouldn't be there by—"

"How long are they staying?" he interrupted.

"Until Isaac gets out of jail."

"And when will that be?"

I shrugged.

"Well, you get to clean up after them."

I frowned. "Valerie and Cody aren't puppies."

"After you chase that two year old around for a few days, you'll wish they were," he said, attaching a padlock to the chain. He turned to me smiling. Thurman had taken the news better than I'd expected. He was probably relieved I hadn't mortgaged the house to bail Isaac out.

"By the way," he said. "Mrs. Lyttle gave me a sack of vegetables when I fixed her fence. I put it on the kitchen counter."

"Maybe you should take that chain off and put the wire back on," I suggested. "Letting Blue get into her garden pays off. Was Mrs. L paying you for fixing the fence our horse broke, or did you take off your shirt while you were working and show off your manly chest?"

He laughed. "I kept my shirt on."

"I bet she was disappointed," I said. "I would have been."

"I'll take my shirt off for you tonight. But it will be late. Luis and I are leaving for Houston right after lunch."

"You're going to deliver the chairs *today?*" I asked. He and Luis had been putting the finishing touches on a set of chairs for the First United Methodist Church in Houston. "I thought you weren't delivering them until next week?"

"They're ready. Luis called the pastor. He's anxious to have them delivered. Besides, Monika's out of town visiting her mother, so there's no reason for Luis to rush home. And I figured you'd be needing a nap after last night." He pointed toward the back door where Valerie was emerging with Cody in tow. "Looks like you won't be getting one now." He bent to pick up a bag of staples, then together, we walked over to Val and Cody.

"Hi, Mr. Matheson. Thanks for letting us stay with you."

"Sure thing," Thurman said, holding his hands out to Cody who ran and jumped into his arms.

"This is so cool," Valerie said, looking around. "Look, Cody." She pointed. "A cow."

"Actually. That is a bull," I said.

"But it doesn't have horns."

"Horns don't make a bull. Another part of the anatomy makes it a bull."

She looked puzzled for a moment, then the light bulb came on. She blushed.

"We'll have lessons on farm animals later, Val. Let's go see the chairs Luis and Thurman built."

As we entered the workshop, Luis looked up from the computer, waved, then turned back to concentrate on whatever he was working on. Thurman led us to the chairs made of purple heart and black walnut. The backs were carved in a design of an Easter Lily bouquet.

"Oh! They're so pretty," Valerie said. "How did you do this?"

"This is Luis' project," Thurman said.

"They're beautiful, Luis," I said.

"Thanks," Mr. Bashful said, not turning away from the computer.

"They're too beautiful to sit on," Valerie said.

"They'll be sat on. They're going in the vestibule of the church. They *are* strong enough. Think of our furniture as usable art." He motioned with his free hand. "Go ahead. Sit on it."

Valerie hesitated a moment, but with Thurman's nod, she sat down and leaned back slowly. She looked up at me. "I didn't think it would be comfortable, but it is."

Thurman grinned proudly. "Hear that Luis? You've got a future customer."

Luis waved without looking up.

"Come on," Thurman said. "I'll show you the rest." He led us around the workshop, showing off the other projects he and Luis were working on, until Cody started squirming, trying to get down. "Not in here, you little rascal. There's too much for you to get into." He handed the wiggle worm to me.

"Come on, Val. Let's fix some lunch for these men so they can be on their way."

~~~

While I slapped together sandwiches, and Val prepared finger foods for Cody, he delighted in chasing the cats around the kitchen and dining room. Agatha was none too pleased and beat a hasty retreat to another part of the house. A tolerant and teasing Melrose sauntered just out of Cody's reach, stopped long enough for Cody to catch up and grab
~~~

him around the middle, then as the child struggled to lift the huge beast, he wriggled from Cody's grasp. This game continued until Val plucked up the terrible not-quite twoster, washed his hands, and sat him down at the table.

About that time Thurman stuck his head in the door and asked me to pack his and Luis's lunch so they could get on their way. I wrapped their sandwiches, tossed them, some high-fat-high-cholesterol snacks, and sodas in a sack then delivered the sacks to the men who were loading the last of the chairs in the back of the delivery van.

Thurman pulled down the van's overhead door, took the sacks, and kissed me good-bye. "It'll take a good three hours to get to the church. We probably won't be home until after dark."

"Especially if we stop off at Kraatz's Bar-B-Q on the way home," Luis said as he climbed in the passenger's side.

"If you do, you'd better bring some of their spare ribs and mustard potato salad home," I said.

I returned to the house. Cody was already in the playing stage of eating. Val looked exhausted. We ate lunch with little conversation, most of it coming from Valerie describing Isaac's confrontation with the police. If it occurred as she described, the police goaded Isaac, and Isaac being Isaac reacted exactly the way they'd hoped he would.

Cody yawned, starting a chain reaction through Val and then me.

"I'll clean up," I said. "You need to get the baby down for a nap. You might want to take one with him."

"You don't mind?" she asked, rising.

"We all had very little sleep last night. I'm going to make some calls then lie down myself."

Fighting a strong inclination to flop down on the sofa and sleep until bedtime, I phoned Willemina as I cleared the table with my free hand.

"What have you found out?" I asked when she answered.

"Hi, Darby. Not much. I didn't want to call anyone too early. Most people want to sleep in on Saturday, especially if they've been up late partying. When it was a resonable hour to start phoning, Richard woke up and requested bacon and eggs to go with the peach buns before he headed off to the golf course. I've been able to reach only six people."

"How many are on the list?" I asked.

"Five hundred."

"Five hundred?!?"

"I printed the guest list from last night."

"Cripes." It was going to take forever. "Okay," I said. "Fax a copy of the list to me and one to Ariana. You take the first two hundred, and Ariana and I will split the final three hundred."

"May I ask why I have to make most of the calls?"

"Because you like to talk."

"I don't like to talk that much," she said flatly.

"Maybe we won't have to call everyone on the list." *Lord,* I hoped not. I wouldn't describe myself as shy, but I draw a line at butting into someone else's business. "Mind your own beeswax" is the motto I choose to live by, so *how* did I manage to paint myself into interrogating one hundred and fifty strangers? "How am I supposed to talk to these people?" I asked.

"Oh, you know, just conversation. Thank you for your support ... it went well at least until Claire Nathe went missing ... isn't it awful about her death...."

"And no one is offended by your snooping?"

"*I* don't snoop. I am merely interested."

"*Excuse me.* How many have been 'interested' back?"

"Four. Betty Ainsworth had heard about Claire's death, but she also knew about the confrontation with Isaac, so she has already tried and convicted him. Ken Amayo said it was too bad, but he wasn't surprised that someone finally had had all they could stand of Claire."

I began loading the dishwasher. "What did he mean by that?"

"He didn't say. Do you want his number?"

"I sure do."

"Darby, do you think we're handling this correctly?"

"How else are we going to handle it?" I asked.

"I don't know. Maybe we should take a course in investigating techniques."

"We don't have time for a course. Besides, you can get gossip out of a dead turnip."

"Thanks. But the idiom is 'blood out of a turnip.'"

"You're good at that, too. Keep calling people. I'll talk Ariana into helping. Sooner or later, we'll find out something that will clear Isaac."

Chapter Twelve

After we said good-bye, I called Ariana, who didn't bother to say hello. She got right to the point. "Dawson is definitely having an affair."

I sighed.

"Well, say something."

"If you were *certain* he was fooling around, and not just suspicious, you wouldn't be announcing it in that way."

The green-eyed monster in Ariana had grown barely controllable after dating, living with, and marrying a string of skunks over the years. It didn't take much to encourage her jealousy, which in the past had been very much justified, but in this case, I knew she was wrong, so I did my best to quell the beast.

"I have proof," she said.

"Real proof or circumstantial?"

"Real. I found a real estate guide for Waco on his desk."

"So?"

"You know we have an apartment in Waco. We leased

it when Dawson contracted to direct the Waco Symphony."

Dawson burns up the road splitting his time between Dulcinea and Waco. While being away from Ariana's scrutiny could give him opportunity, I didn't believe he had the desire. First off, he loves his wife, and secondly, he knows how she's been hurt in the past, and thirdly, he's not a skunk.

"Maybe he doesn't like the apartment." *Highly unlikely considering Ariana's good taste and unlimited bank account.* "Maybe he's shopping around for a better place. Did you ask him?"

"No, I'm not going to let him think I'm suspicious."

"But you are suspicious."

"Why aren't you taking this seriously?"

"Because I don't think Dawson is being unfaithful. Besides, we've got bigger fish to fry. Isaac was arrested for Claire's murder."

"You are kidding."

"I've been up since seven-thirty. Val and the baby are staying with us, and I need your help."

"I don't do babies."

Ariana is the oldest of eight kids. When she went off to college, she left child care responsibilities far behind with no inclination of picking them up again in the future. The closest she's ever come to motherhood is pampering her Lhasa Apso, Chispa.

"I'm not asking you to keep Val and Cody," I said.

"You bet you're not. If I had to watch a kid, I'd have to double my Xanax," she said. "Why didn't you see this coming? You spent ten minutes with Isaac after he got in the fight with Claire. Why didn't you see?"

I tried to recall what I was feeling when I talked to Isaac yesterday afternoon. Concern. Disappointment. But *bug guts?* No. No *bug guts.* "Because he didn't do it," I said.

"Are you certain your radar didn't get scrambled? Isaac's little family is one of your favorites."

"I'll admit my feelings get a little distorted when it comes to those I care about, but I did not have one twinge of *bug guts* when I spoke to him."

"That's real dependable. Like you didn't have a twinge of *bug guts* about Dawson."

"Give me a break, and give Dawson one, too. I want you to make some phone calls. Willemina has already started calling the party-goers. She's also working on a name for our little detective agency."

"Agency?"

"All right. Our group."

"Group? Don't you mean pair?"

"No. I mean 'group.' Willi, me, and you."

"Oh, no. Keep me out of this imbecilic escapade. I have enough to deal with without getting caught up in your fantasies. Besides, what do you know about conducting an investigation?"

"I'm a librarian for crying out loud. Do you know how many times students have walked into my library and said, 'I need a book'? That's what I get to start with. 'I need a book.' My job for the past twenty-five years has been to discover exactly what that child needed, and I did it by asking questions. Often times, it wasn't even a book they needed. Sometimes, they needed a magazine article, a directory, a CD, or to search the web. Sometimes they were just trying to skip class. But I didn't find that out until I started asking questions."

"That doesn't make you a detective," she said. "And what about Willi and me? We don't know the first thing about being private eyes."

"We are not going into business. We are helping Isaac. I know how to ask questions because of years in the library. Willemina knows half this town and can find out about the other half through her connections. Your fame works in your favor. All you have to do is say 'This is Ariana,' and people are falling all over you. Isaac needs your help. The police think they have the killer, but you know Isaac couldn't do such a thing."

"I don't know Isaac at all. For all I know, he may very well have killed Claire in a fit of rage."

"That's my point—*in a fit of rage,* maybe he could have done it, but Claire's murder was plotted and planned. Someone coaxed her into the arena and strangled her with a belt that had more than one set of fingerprints on it."

"How do you know that?" Ariana asked.

"The chief told me. As a matter of fact, he fingerprinted me."

"He what?"

"He fingerprinted me when I told him my prints were probably on the belt. And you know what? They were. They got a match of my right thumb and pinkie."

"You are kidding, right?"

"No, really. Remember when I picked up those things that fell from the Fronds and Feathers rack as it was being brought in, and I got *bug guts*? I was holding the murder weapon, except it wasn't yet the murder weapon."

"Ayyye, de tu madre." I could picture Ariana crossing herself and looking heavenward.

I ignored her exasperation. "So you see, the same thing could have happened with Isaac, except I don't know when he touched the belt, because I can't talk to him until Monday."

"Is that when he's getting out?"

"Not unless you want to cough up twenty-five thousand dollars."

"I think I'll pass."

"Look, the chief said Dulcinea PD is hit with more than thirty new crimes a day, the department has a shortage of officers, and they have enough evidence on Isaac to make a case. That means the police will not be spending any more time looking for someone else. It's up to us. So my question to you is, are you in?"

Before she could answer, I heard a hum coming from down the hall. "Hold on. I'm going to check the fax machine," I said as I walked to the guest room which doubles for an office. "Go see if your copies have come through."

"What copies?"

"Willi should be sending you the list of attendees."

"I don't have time to make—"

"Oh, good," I said, ignoring her protest. "Willemina marked the list. It looks like she'll contact everyone above 'Mr. and Mrs. Mark Gossett.' You phone from the Gossetts down to...." I counted off approximately 150 names. "Mr. and Mrs. Michael Perry. I'll call the rest."

"Do you realize how long it will take to call that many people?"

"I don't think we'll have to. Once we heat up the phone lines and people know we want dirt on Claire, they'll start calling us."

"Has it occurred to you, my brilliant friend, that if someone other than Isaac killed Claire—"

"Isaac didn't kill Claire," I said.

"Would you let me finish, please?"

"Go ahead."

"If someone other than Isaac killed Claire, that someone might not like our snooping around?"

I got that bug-crawling-up-the-back-of-my-neck feeling.

"There you go, getting all melodramatic again," I said. "We'll be perfectly safe."

Chapter Thirteen

Fortunately, Willemina's list was complete—with names, addresses, and telephone numbers. Unfortunately, I was not well-acquainted with many people on my portion of the list, or with many on *any* portion of the list. Until recently, my social group consisted of educators, students, and some parents. The patrons of Dulcinea's social events were a tad outside my normal social realm, but if I had learned nothing else about hobnobbing with the "haves" over the last few years of helping with charity functions, I had learned how to name-drop.

Mr. and Mrs. Edward Persilver were the first on my list. After Mrs. Persilver answered, I introduced myself as the chairwoman of the decorating committee for last night's European Rhapsody benefit for the Dulcinea Performing Arts Center, and I was calling "on behalf of Mrs. Richard Henry and Mrs. Dawson Wu, of course, you know them as Willemina and Ariana, to ask your impression of the event and how we might improve it next year ..." and eventually asking had she heard the terrible news about Claire Nathe.

One would expect from a select group of people, those willing and able to spend money on building a performing arts center, that more would know each other. Of course, I'm not talking about myself. I know, of the nearly one thousand people in attendance last night, I am the most likely to blend into the wallpaper, but I thought, surely, these people would know Willemina or Ariana or Claire. Name-dropping worked on a few. However, I was having the same rotten luck as Willi. Either they didn't answer the phone, didn't know Claire, didn't or wouldn't share any personal information about Claire, or they had arrived at the same conclusion as the police.

I was about eight calls along when I remembered Ken Amayo. He *had* had something negative to say about Claire to Willemina, he just didn't say enough. I wanted to know what he meant by "finally someone had had all they could stand of Claire." I dialed his number, and it was answered on the second ring.

"Hello." It was a woman's voice.

"Mrs. Amayo? This is Darby Matheson," I said, going into my opening spiel.

When I had finished, Mrs. Amayo said, "We had a wonderful time last night. The style show was great fun. Our daughter, Jaclyn, was one of the models. Do you remember seeing her? She wore the gold brocade vest over a white silk shirt with black leather pants."

I had been more interested in the show than the style of the style show, so I lied. "Yes. Of course. She's a lovely girl."

"Thank you. We're very proud of her."

"Mrs. Amayo, I know Willemina Henry spoke to your husband earlier today about Claire Nathe's death. Did he mention their conversation?"

"Yes," she said, followed by an uncomfortable length of silence.

It seemed I'd slammed the door on her chattiness. I hoped I could wedge it open again. "Mrs. Amayo, I don't like to gossip, but Willemina seems to think your husband had, let's say, a less-than-positive experience with Claire. Not that it surprises me, mind you. I was subjected to Claire's *unusual* personality myself."

Her bubbly voice went flat. "You mean unpleasant. And call me Esme."

Aaaah! Success. "Well, Esme," I broke into my best I-wouldn't-want-to-speak-ill-of-the-dead-but voice. "Everyone has a bad day now and then, and one doesn't deserve to die just because they are unpleasant, but last year during the Lung Association benefit, Claire was absolutely horrible to Ariana. She practically blackmailed her into...." I went on to describe Ariana's run-in with Claire and Willemina's inability to reason with her.

"She's a bitch," Esme said. "Or *was.* Let me tell you what she did to my daughter."

Fifteen minutes later, I had three people who had as much or more motive as Isaac to want Claire dead—Ken, Esme, and Jaclyn Amayo.

Chapter Fourteen

If anyone ever needs to torture me for information, sleep deprivation is the way to go. I could handle bamboo shoots under the fingernails better than I could handle going without REM. Even though Esme's disclosure opened up a realm of scenarios, I was too punch drunk from having only three hours of shut eye to think straight.

I made my way to the bedroom where Thurman had thoughtfully made the bed. (Why is it when a man makes the bed once every four months, wives consider it thoughtful?) I kicked off my shoes and crawled on top of the comforter. I don't remember closing my eyes, but remember something about baby pigs squealing and running around a muddy pen. When I opened my eyes, the clock read: 6:18, and the pigs were still making noise, but now they were in the hallway. I opened the bedroom door to find Cody chasing Sawdust down the hall toward me, with Valerie following closely behind trying to hush them. Goldens are good-natured kid dogs, and Sawdust enjoyed the gleeful toddler hanging onto his neck, as was evidenced by the whacking of his wagging tail along the walls.

"I'm sorry Cody woke you," Valerie said.

"That's all right," I said, with a yawn. "I didn't realize it was so late. I need to get up and get some things done."

Val straightened a picture on the wall. "Are these your kids?"

I pointed to the two individual portraits of my children in their caps and gowns. "That's Marissa. She's twenty-six now. That is Samuel. He's twenty-four."

She noticed the next picture. "Who's that in the uniform?"

"That's Sam. He's a pilot in the U.S. Navy."

"That looks like Marissa," she said, pointing to a snapshot of my daughter in her nun's habit.

"It is." Looking at the pictures reminded me of the undeveloped film in my purse. The pictures I took at the benefit could contain a clue to Claire's murder, or they could prove Isaac's innocence. I was thinking I probably should turn the undeveloped film over to the police when Valerie said, "I didn't know you were Catholic."

"I'm not. It's a long story. I have to go back into town." I led the way to the kitchen. "Do you need anything at the grocery store?"

"Ummm, no. But would you mind taking me back to my house? I forgot Cody's nebulizer. He hasn't had an asthma attack for a while, but he needs to take his medicine regularly. I was so worried about Isaac, I forgot it. I'm sorry to be so much trouble."

"You're not. If you don't mind letting me have your key, I'll swing by your house. I can be home before dark, and you won't have to load and unload the baby."

"You don't mind?" she asked.

"Not at all. You can take Cody outside to see the animals. Just don't let him get between a cow and her calf. Some of our cows are very protective, and some are just plain mean."

~~~

The newspaper listed sunset at 8:07 P.M. It was a quarter to seven before I finally left the house, but I could make it to the grocery store, Val's, back to pick up the photos, and still get home before it was totally dark around eight-thirty. I ran into the store, dropped off seven rolls of film at the film counter (Lord knows what happened to the eighth. After Claire's body was discovered I was lucky to have remembered to retrieve my camera), asked for one hour developing, then dashed to the back to pick up cat food where I ran into the first snag.

I've heard women speak 5,000 words a day while men use only 2,000. Thurman stockpiles at least 1,500 a day, which is considerate of him because I used my allocation *and* his.

From the Tidy Cat to the Mrs. Baird's Whole Wheat, I talked with friends and acquaintances, none of whom were helpful to our investigation, about the murder of Claire Nathe. By the time I made it to the checkout counter, it was seven forty-five. Crap! How did I waste so much time just dropping off film? Now I was down to three-quarters of an hour of light. No sweat. I could make it to Valerie's in fifteen minutes.
~~~

Chapter Fifteen

Long shadows covered the street when I arrived at her house. I sat in the Suburban with the doors locked surveying in all directions before opening the door and stepping out. I locked my purse in the Suburban, carried my keys and Val's, and negotiated the broken steps. As I reached for the door knob, a strong wave of *bug guts* hit me. *I'm going to have to start carrying Pepto-Bismol,* I thought.

If it had been as easy as picking up a bottle of Children's Tylenol at the store, I would have done it, but the asthma medicine was a prescription and had to be placed in a special tubing attached to a machine that vaporized the liquid making it easy for the baby to inhale. Everything I needed was on the other side of the front door, so I swallowed the warning and went in.

I walked through the living area, found the light switch just inside the kitchen door, and flipped it on. An old refrigerator was just to my left—next, a rusted dinette table with two chairs that were minus their padding. A door leading into the back yard was just beyond the table. The security chain hung loose, so I fastened it and checked the lock on the doorknob before turning to the counter. The nebulizer was right where Valerie had said it would be. I checked to make sure everything was inside the little suitcase before snapping the cover shut. I turned from the counter to leave and nearly jumped out of my skin. A man stood in the doorway.

"You scared me," I said as if it hadn't been obvious from the gasp that had escaped me.

"Who *are* you?" he asked as if he owned the house.

I couldn't help thinking, I was trapped by a serial killer. I tried to sound black-belt tough. "I'm a friend of Valerie. Who are you?"

"I'm Valerie's daddy."

"You're Mr. Ybarra?" I knew full-well he was not.

Val's father was Hispanic. This guy was Anglo, probably in his early forties, about five-ten with neatly cut hair, square jaw, dimpled chin. Dressed in jeans and a sport shirt, he probably weighed about one-eighty-five. If he hadn't been standing between me and the front door, I might have thought him attractive.

He crossed his arms, leaned against the door jamb and said, "I'm her stepdaddy." A ten pound weight dropped from my throat and landed in my colon.

This was Tony, Val's mother's new boyfriend. The same Tony that made Val uncomfortable. My initial judgment had not been far off the mark. He may not be a serial killer, but he was making me very uncomfortable, too. I was mentally kicking myself for coming here alone while doing cerebral acrobatics trying to figure out a way to talk my way past Tony, out of the house, and into the safety of my locked vehicle.

I decided to continue the blissfully ignorant and overly polite route. "It's nice to meet you, Mr...?"

"Where is Valerie?"

"She's staying with me for a few days." Forcing a smile, I looked around the kitchen as if making sure I hadn't forgotten anything. "Well, I'd better get going."

"What's your hurry?"

An expression can reveal in an instant what one spends a lifetime to hide, though I doubted Tony cared what he revealed at that moment. His expression told me he held me in contempt. That he enjoyed making me uncomfortable. His expression had me wishing for pepper spray—or a handgun. His expression and tone of voice pushed me past uncomfortable and into frightened. I glanced toward the back door where the security chain had me safely locked *in*. I held the nebulizer in front of myself like a shield. "The baby needs his breathing treatment," I said. My voice revealed my fear, but I couldn't control it.

"He can wait."

He took one step toward me, and my counterfeit courage completely shattered. "You better leave. Valerie told me about you," I squeaked.

He continued toward me, talking in a slippery, quiet, unnerving tone. "What did she say? That she likes me? That she *wants* me?"

"She said you make her sick."

His slimy smile became a snarl. "I came here for Valerie. But you'll do." I tried to rush past him as he came toward me, but he grabbed my arm. "I don't think so."

"Let me go!" I screamed, trying to grasp the nebulizer in my free hand so that I could pull it back to use as a weapon. Tony twisted me around so that he stood behind me, holding both of my arms against the case and pulling it up and into my breasts. The pain he inflicted was minor compared to the terror of what I imagined would be next. I struggled trying to unbalance him, but it only caused him to laugh.

"Oooh, baby. Yeah. That feels good. Do that some more," he said.

I screamed, and Tony's hand came up to cover my mouth.

"Let her go," a voice said.

My attacker swung me around, so he could look over my shoulder into the darkened living room.

Jerome Steele is the color of a Hershey's Special Dark Chocolate in the daylight and nearly invisible at night. I could not see his face, but his voice and blessedly large shape was as welcome as a SWAT team.

"Oh. Thank God," I breathed.

"Let her go," he said again. I heard a click and saw light bounce off the blade in Jerome's hand. Even from a distance and in the dark, I knew it wasn't a pocket knife he was holding. So did Tony. He released me, and I ran to Jerome's side—the side that wasn't holding the switchblade.

"Chill, homes," Tony said. "We're just having a little conversation here."

"Your 'conversation' is over." Jerome started toward Tony.

"No, Jerome," I said. "Let him go. I don't want you to get in trouble on my account. Besides," I laughed nervously. "You don't want to get blood all over Valerie's kitchen do you?"

He stopped in mid-stride giving Tony time to run for the back door, throw off the chain, and bolt down the steps. Jerome continued across the room and looked out the open door. Satisfied that Tony was long gone, he closed the door and re-locked it.

He turned around to face me as he closed his knife and pocketed it. "Mrs. Matheson, you shouldn't be down here alone."

"Lapse in judgment," I said.

"I'll walk you to your vehicle."

When we reached the Suburban, I asked, "What were you doing here?"

"I drove by, recognized your SUV, knew Isaac was picked up this morning. Figured you were checking on Valerie. Thought I'd stick around, just in case."

"But you don't live here. What were you doing in this neighborhood?" I asked, knowing the answer before I asked it.

"Just business," he said.

"What kind of business?"

"A very lucrative business, Mrs. Matheson. Go home. Be safe."

You'd think that after nearly being raped and killed by a psycho, I'd be happy to do as Jerome said, but the teacher in me couldn't quit lecturing. "I wish you would think about college. You've got the intelligence and grades to be anything you want. You've got to start making better choices, Jerome."

"Yes, Ma'am." He opened the driver's door. "So do you."

I couldn't argue with that.

Chapter Sixteen

I made it as far as the first brightly lit parking lot of a store that didn't need burglar bars on its plate glass windows before I started shaking so badly that I had to pull over. My mind replayed over and over being trapped in the kitchen, struggling against that creep's aroused body, with him saying "that feels good. Do that some more." I felt repulsed, angry, afraid, ashamed, helpless. I don't know how long I sat in the parking lot, but I had a good, long, racking-sobs cry before I pulled myself together and drove home.

When I walked in the house, Cody was sound asleep in Valerie's arms. She rose from Thurman's rocker-recliner. Carrying the nebulizer, I followed her to the guest room.

"Did you have any problems finding it?" she asked.

I shook my head. She didn't need to know the problem I had. "I'm kind of wiped out though," I said. "I think I'll hit the sack. If you need extra towels, they're in the hall closet. Make yourself at home."

"Thanks, Mrs. Matheson. You're an angel."

I smiled, then went into my bedroom for another cry.

Thurman came home at eleven-o-six. I know, because I had been staring at the alarm clock since I'd crawled into bed. I pretended to be asleep when he came in the room, because I didn't want him to know what had happened.

Logic told me to tell my husband I'd been assaulted. But I discovered logic was a misty illusion compared with the reality of attempted rape. I couldn't talk to him about it. When my bear of a husband crawled into bed and wrapped his arms around me, I finally felt safe. Long after he fell into the rhythmic breathing of sleep, I slept, too.

~~~

I awoke before everyone else, dressed in faded shorts and a paint-splattered shirt, gathered bucket, rags, cleaners, and paper towels and attacked the dirt, dust, and grime in the family room which is located at the far end of the house.

Cleaning is not my hobby. It is something I do when company is expected, when Thurman, who is not a clean freak, starts to complain about a dirty house, or when I am stressed. I must have been living a calm existence for quite a while; when I'd finished, the rags were filthy, I'd gone through a complete roll of paper towels, and the bucket held sludge. But I could actually see through the windows, the baseboards were dust free, the corners were no longer spider web subdivisions, and the wood furniture gleamed.

I had started organizing the pantry when I heard a toilet flush in the other end of the house. I wasn't sure if it was Thurman or Valerie who was awake, but I stopped organizing and took the box of instant pancakes off the shelf. I was feeling almost normal by the time we were all seated around the breakfast table.

That is, until Valerie started crying. "He didn't do it. I know he didn't do it. We can't afford a lawyer. What if Isaac goes to prison? What am I going to do? I don't want my baby growing up without his daddy."
~~~

Thurman reached over and patted her hand. "Don't worry, kiddo. We'll take one day at a time."

She looked up at him. "You're being so nice to me, Mr. Matheson, letting me stay here." She turned to me. "And buying the diapers, and going all the way back to my house last night to get the nebulizer."

Thurman frowned. "You did what?"

"I went to Valerie's house to get the baby's asthma medicine," I said nonchalantly.

Valerie seemed to be aware of the sudden change in Thurman. "It's my fault," she said. "I forgot Cody's medicine."

Thurman didn't look her way. He was too busy glaring at me. "You were in Pleasant Valley after dark? It's not safe in that part of town. Isn't that why you brought Valerie here? And then you turn around and *go back!* What were you thinking?"

I didn't say a word. If I had, I would have blurted out everything. I didn't want to break down, and I didn't want Thurman going *Die Hard.* Not that I didn't want Tony dead. I didn't feel good about wanting him dead, but that's the truth of the matter. He scared me. I didn't want that slime to hurt me, and I didn't want him to hurt Valerie and, *for God's sake,* I didn't want him to hurt Cody. Along with horrible rape scenes pin balling around in my head, I saw Thurman grabbing his .45, hunting down Tony, and pumping him full of lead. Then I saw Thurman sitting on the bottom bunk while Isaac sat on the top bunk in a Huntsville State Prison cell.

"It's not safe," Thurman repeated.

"Which is why we need to find a safe place for these kids to live when Isaac gets out. And he will get out, because, like Valerie said, 'he didn't do it.'"

Thurman shook his head. "You're changing the subject. Promise me you will not go to that part of town after dark. And if you must go during the day, you'll take someone with you."

"I didn't plan on being there after dark. When I left here, I thought I had plenty of time. But it took longer in the grocery store than I'd planned and the time got away from me."

"Promise."

"I promise." *Bruce.*

The previous day, solving Claire Nathe's murder was more like solving a puzzle. A very important puzzle. After all, if we could prove that Isaac was innocent, he would get out of jail and all would be right with the world. Valerie and Isaac were important to me. They weren't just my students, they were kids to whom I'd grown very close. But in my heart, proving Isaac's innocence had been just a puzzle. Last night changed that. It turned on a light for me that exposed the cockroaches and venomous creatures infecting Valerie's and Isaac's and Cody's lives. I had to do everything I could to help them.

After breakfast, Valerie cleaned up the kitchen while I made a few phone calls to inquire about Claire. Most people were leaving for church or not at home. The ones I did talk to didn't shed any new light on the situation, so I gave up and spent the morning doing chores. Valerie needed to wash clothes, then she vacuumed while I dusted and cleaned bathrooms. Sawdust, the cats, and some toys kept Cody entertained, but when he showed an interest in trying to plug in the vacuum cleaner, I made a note to buy safety plugs for the electrical sockets along with a few child safety locks for the cabinets. Thurman spent the morning making repairs on the barn.

After we had lunch, I told Thurman I had errands to run in town, and I'd probably swing by Ariana's house. He was going to take a nap, then do some more chores. Valerie said she and the baby would be okay left on their own. Cody was ready for a nap, and she needed to catch up on her schoolwork.

~~~

The Wu's home sits a few miles west of town in a prime wooded area overlooking the river. In the past twenty years, the hundred-year-floods seemed to have hit every three or four years, but Ariana's and Dawson's house was built high on a hill. A flood might cover the road leading to their place, but only one of Noah's magnitude would get near the house.

The house itself is a Mediterranean villa with columned porch, arched and circular windows, a clay tile roof, and large enough to house all of Ariana's brothers and sisters and their families if Ariana ever had such an inclination, which is very doubtful.

When Ariana's housekeeper Dee opened the door, Chispa bounced up and down begging to be picked up. She thanked me by trying to lick the peach fuzz off my chin. Dee told me "Miss Ariana" was in the greenhouse then led me through the house to the sliding back door.

I made my way around the pool, stopping to admire Ariana's recent art acquisition—a bench carved from a solid piece of white marble, the back of the bench shaped like a dove with outstretched wings. I continued down the stone steps to the greenhouse and found her with her gloved hands troweling soil into a flower pot amid hundreds of blooming orchids.

"How's it going?" I asked.

She shrugged. "Don't put the dog down. She'll get filthy."

How Ariana managed to keep the white shirt and overalls clean while shoveling potting soil amazed me. I patted Chispa's head. She seemed content to stay cradled in my arms. "You're still mad at Dawson?"

"It's over," she said, concentrating on getting every soil particle settled in its rightful place in the pot.

"'It's over' your anger is over, or 'it's over' your marriage is over?"
~~~

"I found a check made out to the Brisa de Verano Apartments. I called information for Waco. Then I called the number the operator gave me and asked to speak to the manager. I told her I was Mrs. Dawson Wu and my husband had asked me to have maintenance fix the garbage disposal. She put me on hold. When she came back on the line, she said they had no tenant by the name of Dawson Wu."

"You think she's lying?"

"I *know* Dawson rented an apartment there. I saw the canceled check."

"I can't believe Dawson is fooling around."

Ariana snatched off her gloves and threw them on the table. "Come with me." She stalked past me, out the door and up the stone steps. I had no choice but to follow in her fiery wake.

When we entered the living room, I set the dog on the floor. Chispa bounced across the white carpet to take the lead. Most of the house is decorated in shades of white and an unusual but esthetically pleasing blend of Asian, Latin American, and Modern art. A Julian Stanczak original, taking up most of the living room wall toward which we walked, usually made me dizzy every time I looked at it. In order to keep up with Ariana, I hurried past it through the sliding double doors leading into Dawson's office.

There's no white carpeting in here. The floor is wood; the walls are solid walnut wood paneling. A grand piano takes up part of the room. Dawson's cello, stationed behind a music stand holding sheet music, rests to the left of the paper-littered desk which sits upon a Harley Davidson wool rug. A Harley Davidson lamp sits atop the desk, a Harley Davidson upholstered executive chair sits behind it, and a Harley Davidson clock adorns the wall directly behind that.

"Where's Dawson?" I asked.

"In Waco," she said icily.

Probably got there on his Harley, I thought.

Ariana shifted a pile of papers to reveal an answering machine. She pushed play, then forwarded through a few messages. Eventually, she found the message she was searching for. A young woman's voice said, "Hello, Dawson. This is *biao mei* Lily. The apartment is wonderful. You are so sweet for getting it for me. *Wo ai ni.* See you soon."

Ariana turned off the recorder. Tears pooled in her eyes, but she was too controlled to let them course down her face. "You see? You see? Give me a reasonable explanation for that."

I opened my mouth to speak but nothing came out. The voice on the recorder had a sweet-young-thing quality. The accent was west coast, but she was speaking Chinese—most likely Mandarin.

"Maybe it's time to talk to Dawson," I said.

She walked into Dawson's private bathroom. I heard a Kleenex being snatched out of the box, then Ariana returned with dry eyes. "I'll do better than that. I'll let my lawyer talk to him."

I did not want to believe it was true. Dawson wouldn't treat Ariana like this. He wouldn't cheat on her. "Keep in mind this may be perfectly innocent," I said. "Did you understand everything she said? What does *biao mei* mean?"

"Mistress!"

"It does not."

"I don't know what it means. I don't speak Mandarin." She reached for the phone. "But I know someone who does." She rapidly keyed in a phone number, then looked at me with determination as she waited for an answer.

In a few seconds, she turned away and said in a submissive tone, "Mother Wu. This is Ariana." She spent a few minutes in polite conversation asking about her mother-in-law's health and catching up on family when she finally got to the point. "Dawson isn't here right now. Would you translate something for me?" ... "What does *wo ai ni* mean?" ... "I heard someone use the term and was wondering what it meant." Ariana's shoulders sagged. "A woman," she said impatiently. She listened for a moment then a slight sigh escaped from her before she said, "A woman left a message for Dawson." ... "Oh." Her shoulders sagged even more. "What does *biao mei* mean?" ... "Thank you," Ariana said. Her voice trembled as she said goodbye.

After she hung up the phone, she turned back to me, cleared her throat, and angrily said. *"Biao mei* means 'girlfriend.' *Wo ai ni* is 'I love you.'"

I didn't trust Dawson's mother. She had not been pleased when her oldest son had married outside his race and class. It did not matter to Mrs. Wu that Ariana was a wealthy woman. She had come from a working class, non-Chinese family and was a divorced woman. The last time Ariana and Dawson had visited Mrs. Wu at her home in Houston, Ariana stepped out of the room for a moment and reentered just as Dawson's mother asked him, "why did you have to marry a tall, ugly American when you could have your choice of beautiful Chinese women?" Dawson put his mother in her place, telling her that Ariana *was beautiful,* and she was his wife, so his mother better get use to it and start treating Ariana respectfully or he would stop coming to see her.

"I thought you were never going to speak to Dawson's mother again," I said.

"I got over it." Ariana replayed the message. This time we filled in the Mandarin with English.

"Hello, Dawson. This is *your girlfriend* Lily. The apartment is wonderful. You are so sweet for getting it for me. *I love you.* See you soon."

"As incriminating as it sounds, my intuition is telling me Dawson is innocent," I said.

"And mine is telling me, *he's not.*"

"You, my friend, never listen to your intuition. If you did, it would have told you to avoid Danny in high school, Peter in college, André in Paris, Guiermo in Milan, and let's not forget Kevin in New York."

"You don't have to remind me of my past mistakes."

"I'm trying to keep you from making another one," I stressed. "You believed all of those men were wonderful even while they were two-timing you, living off of you, stealing you blind, or all of the above."

"I'm not going to let it happen again. I'm tired of being played the fool."

"Maybe you are so tired of being played the fool, that you're imagining you're being played the fool." I threw my hands up in the air. "I'm fighting a losing battle here. But one more thing before I give up. If it was me, I'd trust Dawson before I'd trust his mother."

Her expression changed from rage to uncertainty, and I could tell I'd finally gotten her attention. "Before you start throwing Dawson's possessions on the front lawn, talk to *him*." I turned toward the door and started to walk out of the office. "Make me a cup of coffee. I had a rough night last night."

Chapter Seventeen

We were seated on the covered patio next to the swimming pool. A ceiling fan stirred the air and water splashed down the rock waterfall on the far side of the pool as we waited for Dee to serve coffee.

Watching the ripples float across the water's surface, I felt myself relax with each tiny wave. *If I could just spend the whole day like this,* I thought. The tranquility lasted only a moment longer than the thought.

"What was so bad about last night?" Ariana asked. "Did the little rugrat cry all night?"

I discuss almost everything with Ariana, and have since college. What I won't talk to her about, I'll tell Willemina, but I didn't want to think about what had happened at Valerie's house, much less talk about it. "No," I said. "Cody is no trouble. And it's nice having Valerie around. She's a good kid."

"So, why did you have a rough night?"

I shook my head. "It's over. I'd rather not talk about it.

But I would like to talk to you about how we are going to clear Isaac."

Dee came up quietly behind us to set coffee cups and a dish of pastries on the table between us. We thanked her before she silently disappeared back into the house.

"How do you think you are going to clear Isaac of a murder charge, and I stress the word *you*," Ariana said.

"*We* are going to continue talking to anyone who knew Claire. For example, Willi called Ken Amayo yesterday morning," I said. "He told her, and I'm quoting Willie quoting Ken, 'someone finally had had all they could stand of Claire.' I called Ken's house and spoke to his wife Esme. She said their daughter modeled for you in the style show."

Chispa, who had been dancing on her hind legs begging for a treat, landed in my lap and helped herself to the glazed croissant in my hand.

"Stop feeding the dog," Ariana said.

I scowled at her. "Do you remember Jaclyn?"

"Yes. She was really nervous at first, but she did quite well. She's a sweet girl."

"She had a summer job working for Gary for a few weeks this summer."

"Really?"

"According to Esme, Claire had it in for Jaclyn from the start. She made her life miserable until Jaclyn quit work."

"I've had employees who lasted only a few weeks," Ariana said. "They usually have lousy work habits. Arrive at work late, don't show up at all, or come in with a hangover. They quit because they know they're about to be fired. Do you really think Claire had something to do with Jaclyn quitting or is that the story Jaclyn told her parents because she didn't like the job?"

"I don't know. I've never met the girl. But I've met Claire. You know them both. What do you think?"

"Jaclyn probably told the truth. Claire had her own

business to run; why was she interfering with Gary's employee? And what did she *do* to make Jaclyn quit her job?"

"Esme didn't go into detail, but she did say the problem was *Claire,* not Gary, and that they'd had to take Jaclyn to counseling because of whatever Claire pulled. Jaclyn was so upset by what had happened, she was talking about not entering college this fall, but her parents and the counselor convinced her otherwise."

"*Dios mio.* She had to go to a shrink? What in the world did Claire do?"

"I don't know," I said, emphatically. "That's why we need to talk to Jaclyn."

"Why do *I* have to go?"

"I need backup."

"Are you going in with guns blazing?"

"Of course not. But what if she doesn't want to talk to me? You've already built some rapport with her. She may be more comfortable talking to you. Will you go with me?"

"When do you want to go?" she asked, with more than a little lack of enthusiasm.

"What are you doing now?"

~~~

I phoned Willi to ask if she wanted to go with us. She was getting ready to go shopping with Raven but had some suggestions. Ariana and I should pop in unexpectedly, like Peter Falk in *Columbo;* that way, if the Amayos were guilty of anything, they wouldn't have time to get their stories straight.

Ariana rolled her eyes at this. "If I am going to someone's home, I will not be so rude as to just "pop in." If you want to "pop in" on the Amayos, then wait for Willemina to go with you."

I told Willi to enjoy her shopping trip, then waited as Ariana called Esme to ask if it was a convenient time for us to come calling. It was. Ariana changed from her clean,
~~~

white casual work clothes into clean, white casual sports wear, then we took off.

~~~

The Amayo's house was situated on Spanish Grant Circle in Cala Vista, a subdivision designed and built by Ken Amayo Custom Homes. The white two-story Colonial sits on an acre lot surrounded by oaks, esperanzas, and crepe myrtles.

Esmerelda Amayo opened the door. She was probably in her early to mid-forties, a little taller than I, with short black hair, and of average weight. Dressed in brown slacks, an orange and brown print top, and house shoes, she smiled warmly and invited us inside.

"Thank you for letting us come on such short notice," Ariana said as we stepped into the foyer tiled in dark green marble.

"You're very welcome," Esme said, leading us down three steps into a greatroom furnished in overstuffed furniture upholstered in burgundy, green, and gold striped damask. "As I said on the phone, I don't know how we can help. Ken's playing golf this morning, so if you want to talk to him, you'll have to call him at work tomorrow. But Jaclyn said she doesn't mind talking to you, and I'll tell you all I can."

After declining the obligatory invitation of coffee, Ariana and I sat together on a couch facing the floor-to-ceiling windows which overlooked Whitetail Creek, the *cala* in Cala Vista. Esme sat across from us on a matching sofa.

"We apologize for bothering you on a Sunday," I said. You probably have a million things to do, especially with Jaclyn going off to school."

"We have a few more days to get ready, and luckily, we don't have far to go. She's enrolled at the University of Houston and will be staying in the dorm, at least this year, while she gets acclimated to the university environment.
~~~

She's almost packed. She can't take much, because there's not much space in those rooms to begin with. Plus, she'll have a roommate."

"How are you handling the Empty Nest Syndrome?" I asked.

"It's tough, and Jaclyn hasn't even left yet," she said. "She's an only child, which makes her going off to school really rough on me. And after her experience with Claire Nathe, I'm especially apprehensive about her being on her own."

"I'll be all right, Mom."

We turned at the sound of her voice. Jaclyn stood in the entrance to a hallway leading to another part of the house. She was a beautiful girl. Slim, a little taller than her mother, with an oval face, golden brown hair, and light brown eyes. The white denim shorts and hot pink spaghetti strap tee she wore accentuated her tanned skin.

"I don't know if *I'll* be all right," Esme said. "Come say hello."

She came toward us timidly, like a kindergartner meeting her teacher on the first day of school. I could see why Esme was concerned about Jaclyn leaving home. She held out her hand shyly and shook hands with Ariana. "Thanks for letting me be in the style show. It was fun."

"You were a terrific model," Ariana said.

Jaclyn beamed.

"If you were brave enough to walk down a runway in front of all those people at the benefit, I bet you'll be able to handle living on campus. I'm Darby Matheson," I said, extending my hand.

She shook hands and said, "I saw you at the benefit, talking to Ariana when we were in the dressing room. It's nice to meet you." She turned, walked to the other couch, and sat beside her mother.

"Jaclyn is shy, but she works hard to overcome it," Esme explained. "That's why I thought it would be a good idea for her to talk to you about Claire Nathe. When Jaclyn first quit working at Nathe Photography, she wouldn't even leave the house."

"Why do you want to talk about her?" Jaclyn asked.

"Darby thinks that the boy they arrested is innocent, and she has this ridiculous idea that we can prove it," Ariana said, smiling. "Patronize her," she said, cocking her eyes toward me.

"I know Isaac," I said, turning to Ariana. "He didn't kill anyone." I turned back to Jaclyn and Esme. "I think we can get a better idea of who killed Claire if we knew more about her."

"If anyone deserved to get shot, she did," Esme said.

"Mom! They're going to think you did it," Jaclyn said.

"I should have. But I didn't."

"Claire wasn't—" Ariana began. "Ouch!"

"Sorry," I said. "I didn't mean to kick you." I did mean to kick her. She was about to say Claire wasn't shot. But not many people knew that. Even though the murder made the front page of the paper, the cause of death wasn't printed. Ariana needed to watch more crime shows or take investigation lessons like Willi suggested we all do.

I turned back to Jaclyn. "Do you mind telling us what you know about Claire?"

"No. She can't hurt me now, can she?" She reached for her mother's hand. Esme held it in both of hers. "She planted drugs in my desk."

"What?" Ariana blurted.

"Ariana," Jaclyn said, leaning forward, "I was a member of Youth Opposed to Using in high school. I've never used drugs. I don't even smoke." It was obvious she was distressed to think Ariana's opinion of her had changed.

Ariana leaned forward. "*Mija,* I believe you. I'm just shocked that anyone would do such a thing—plant drugs on someone." She shook her head. "Although we *are* talking about Claire. What in the world was she trying to accomplish?"

Jaclyn slumped back into the cushion. "She did accomplish it. She wanted me to quit working for Mr. Nathe."

"Why?"

"Because she was a bitch," Esme said. "I wanted to tear her hair out when I found out what she'd done, but Ken kept me from doing it."

"I would have decked her if she'd done that to one of my kids," I said.

Esme nodded in agreement.

"How did Ken react when he found out?"

"He...." Esme frowned. "You don't suspect one of *us* killed her? Is that why you came over to talk to us?"

Oh, oh. I was moving too fast. I didn't want Esme to stop talking, and I truly didn't think Esme or Jaclyn killed Claire. I didn't know anything about Ken Amayo, so I needed to keep his wife and daughter talking.

"Of course not," I said emphatically. "The only way I can think of to get Isaac out of jail is to find out everything we can about Claire. I want to get a better understanding of who she was. I didn't have a very high opinion of her before we got here, and it's sinking ever lower the more I learn. I certainly don't suspect you or your family of committing murder. But if you could just tell us everything you know, maybe it will put us on the right track. As it is, an innocent kid is sitting in jail. Maybe you can help us get him out."

"We heard that boy was fighting with Claire earlier in the day," Esme said.

"He was," I admitted. I described the incident. "Isaac was just trying to protect his child from Claire."

"I can understand that," Esme said, looking at Jaclyn. She turned back to Ariana and me. "I was very upset when Jaclyn finally told us. I wanted to drive straight over to her house and slap her. Ken was furious. If we had confronted Claire that day, Ken or I could have killed her—but we didn't."

"You didn't confront her? At all?"

"Not in person. Not on the phone."

"You just dropped it?" Ariana asked incredulously.

"No," Esme said. "Ken thinks in terms of business. I wanted to rip into her. He hit her in the wallet."

"What do you mean?"

"He dropped her. Ken occasionally used her company when he'd have an open house. He didn't tell the members of the Dulcinea Builder's Association why he dropped Claire's Concepts from his list of companies to do business with, but he made it very clear to them at the very next meeting that he was no longer using her company for interior decorating. She had already made enemies with some of the other contractors. No one used her at last month's Dulcinea New Homes Tour. As far as I know, all of the building contractors have stopped recommending her services to new home buyers."

"Ken has that much influence?"

"Ken is a respected member of the Builders' Association. But the association is made up of independent contractors, most of whom have built their businesses from the ground up, people who are used to making their own decisions. If one of the other builders was using Claire and happy with her services, Ken's opinion probably wouldn't matter. But if they had never used Claire's Concepts, or if they were considering using another interior decorator, his opinion could cause them to take pause."

"Who 'found' the drugs?" Ariana asked, making little quote marks in the air.

"Claire," Esme said.

"What happened, exactly, Jaclyn?" I asked.

"Gary called me to his office. Mrs. Nathe was there, sitting in Gary's chair behind his desk. Gary asked me to sit down in one of the chairs in front of his desk, and he sat in the other one. He seemed so uncomfortable. He was so nice. I loved working for him," she said as she began to cry.

Esme stood up, walked out of the room, and returned with a box of Kleenex. "I was afraid this would happen."

"We apologize," Ariana said, standing up. "We should never have bothered you. Come on, Darby, let's go," she said, looking down at me.

I ignored her. "Jaclyn, I know this is hard for you. You were accused of something you didn't do. If Claire had called the police and they believed her, you might be behind bars just like Isaac is now. Can you tell us what else happened?"

"It's okay, Mom," Jaclyn said. "I need to talk about it."

Ariana hesitated a moment, then looked at Esme who nodded in assurance. Ariana sat down, and we both waited.

Jaclyn dried her eyes and wiped her nose before she continued. "Mrs. Nathe was just sitting in Gary's chair with this smug look on her face. I knew she was behind whatever was coming." Jaclyn began wringing the tissues in her hand. "Gary showed me a Baggie that held white powder and asked me what it was. I told him I'd never seen it. Mrs. Nathe said I was lying. She'd found it in my desk. I told her it wasn't mine. That I didn't know what it was."

"I notice that you call Gary Nathe, Gary. But you call Claire Nathe, Mrs. Nathe," I said.

She shrugged. "That's what he wanted me to call him. Everyone who comes into the studio calls him Gary. I was too afraid of his wife to address her by anything except Mrs. Nathe."

"That's understandable. What did Gary say when you told him the bag of white powder wasn't yours?"

"He said he believed me. He tried to stand up for me."

"And Claire wasn't satisfied with that?"

"She told Gary his business would be compromised if he continued to let a known drug addict work for him.

I told him I didn't know where the bag came from, that it wasn't mine—that I'd take a drug test to prove it."

"What was in the bag?"

"I don't know," Jaclyn said, twisting the tissues into a thin rope. "I don't know if it was baby powder or flour or cocaine or something. I never found out. Mrs. Nathe said she expected a letter of resignation on Gary's desk within an hour, or she'd call the police. Whether my drug test came out positive or negative, she would tell the police the bag had been in my possession. I was afraid. I didn't know what was in the bag, but I knew Mrs. Nathe would call the police. I had a letter of resignation ready in ten minutes. When I handed the letter to Gary, he apologized to me."

"He believed you, but he thought the bag contained illegal drugs, so he let you resign," I said.

"I think he was trying to protect me."

"He didn't protect you very well," Ariana said. "Why did he let Claire get away with it?"

"I don't know. I didn't understand then. I still don't really understand. I should have gone to work for my dad, but Nathan said his dad was looking for some help in the studio, and I like photography. It's one of my hobbies. I thought I could learn something."

"You know Nathan Nathe?" I asked.

"He was in some of my classes. He knew I took photography as an elective. That's why he mentioned the job opening to me."

"What led up to Claire putting drugs in your desk?"

"She came in one day and said something like, 'if you keep interfering with my family, you'll be sorry.' She was so hateful. I didn't even know what she was talking about."

"Why would she think you were interfering? Were you and Nathan dating?"

"We're just friends." She shook her head, bewildered. "We didn't even talk that much when I was working there.

He's real quiet."

"When you did talk, what did you talk about?"

"Photography. School. You know, starting college in the fall."

"Was he excited about going to Harvard?"

"He didn't seem to be. I don't think it was his first choice. I overheard him and his dad talking one day about MIT. Gary said if that's where he wanted to go, then he should. Nathan said something about needing to keep his mom happy."

"Was that all?" I asked.

She glanced at her mother then back at us. "When I heard Nathan talking about MIT, I said tuition there couldn't be more than tuition at Harvard. He said it wasn't the money. He earned a full academic scholarship. I told him if he earned it, he should be allowed to attend the college of his choice. Nathan said his grandfather had graduated from Harvard, so that's where his mother wanted him to go."

"So Nathan, the sweet boy that he is, would attend a college he didn't want to attend just to keep his mother happy," Ariana said.

"Nathan is sweet," Jaclyn said. "I think he would do anything to keep his mother happy, but not because he's nice. Because he was afraid of her. I got the feeling that Mr. Nathe was afraid of her, too."

Chapter Eighteen

"Why did you kick me?" Ariana asked when we got in the car.

"You were about to spill the beans about the belt used to strangle Claire. There was nothing in the paper about the cause of death, and you shouldn't give out too much information when you're investigating a murder."

"*¡De tu madre!* You sound like you're a private detective. You've been watching too many crime shows."

"If you would stop watching the *novelas* and start watching crime shows, you'd be a better investigator."

"I have no intention of becoming an investigator. I came along to keep you from making a fool of yourself. Now if you will take me home, I've got work to do."

"Like what?"

"Like calling a divorce lawyer."

"Don't jump the gun," I said, starting the car. I pulled out of the driveway and headed back through the neighborhood. "Do you think one of them did it?" I asked.

"Did what?"

"Killed Claire. Do you think one of the Amayos killed Claire? They were all at the benefit. They had the opportunity."

"It's not logical. If one of them had been mad enough to kill her, it would have been the day they learned she planted drugs on Jaclyn."

"That puts them on the same playing field as Isaac."

"Speaking of Isaac, what is happening with him?"

"He'll probably be formally charged tomorrow morning. We'll be able to visit him in the afternoon. I'll probably be able to take Valerie to see him when school lets out."

"You don't think one of them killed Claire, do you?" Ariana asked.

"No," I said, turning onto the highway. "So if it wasn't Isaac, and it wasn't Ken, Esme, or Jaclyn, who killed her?"

We didn't have time to consider the question. *Prelude to the Afternoon of a Faun* rang out from the back seat. "Dig that out of my bag," I said. Ariana twisted around and hauled my purse from behind the driver seat.

"What have you got in here?" she grunted. "Bricks?"

"Everything but. The phone should be in an outside pocket."

It took a moment, but she found it and answered, as I was busy negotiating a left turn.

"Hi, Willemina, this is Ariana. Darby's driving."

"Tell her what we found out at the Amayos'," I said.

Ariana filled Willemina in quickly, accentuating the monologue with a few Spanish swear words underscoring how she felt about Claire. "Can you believe that woman? She tried to ruin that poor girl's life. Jaclyn just wanted a job, for crying out loud, and Claire *Nasty* threatened to have her arrested for something she didn't do."

Ariana listened for a few minutes then said, "hold on." She held the phone away and relayed what Willi said. "Claire's daughter was in Raven's graduating class. Willi said she just dropped Raven off at work, but she wants us to come over tomorrow to talk to Raven and to see her latest project."

Raven is Willemina's and Richard's third daughter. A talented artist, she graduated from high school five years ago, took a job as a checker at a twenty-four-hour grocery store, and never moved out of the house.

Ariana spoke into the phone. "I'll have to see it later. I've got too many calls to make tomorrow. I'm going to open an Ariana V. in Las Vegas.

"You're what?" I screamed.

Ariana held the phone away from her ear again. *"Dios mio.* In stereo."

I could hear Willi's voice across the distance. *"You're going to what?* Las Vegas? How exciting!"

"Are you out of your mind?" I asked.

"Willi? Wait a minute." Ariana glared at me, speaking loud enough that Willi and I both heard her. *"¡Quiese!* If you'll hush, I'll tell you." She waited until Willi's yammering stopped coming through the cell phone earpiece and until she was certain I would shut up and remain silent, then she put the phone back to her ear. "I'm in the preliminary stages, so I do not want either of you breathing a word to anyone, including Dawson."

"You haven't told Dawson?" I asked. Willemina must have asked the same question, because Ariana held the phone away from her ear again.

"No," she said, emphatically. "It's none of his business, and you're not telling him either. You are not to say anything to Richard," she said into the phone, then pointed at me. "And you are not to tell Thurman."

No big deal, I thought. *Since I was keeping something much bigger from him anyway.* "Scout's honor," I said, holding up two fingers. I couldn't remember if scouts held up two fingers or three, or was it four? I'd never been one.

"Are you going to tell us about it?" I asked.

"I started thinking about it after the benefit. I don't have the particulars ironed out, but I'll let you know when I do."

"I thought I heard gears shifting in your brain the other night. Oh!" I gasped. "You're not going to move to Vegas are you?"

"I don't know yet," she said without emotion.

I wanted to scream at her that she couldn't move away. Then I realized she lived here in Dulcinea even though her stores are spread out across Texas. It takes only one more hour to fly to Las Vegas than to drive to Austin. There would be no reason for Ariana to move. That is, if she had no reason to leave her husband. If that stubborn wench wouldn't talk to Dawson, I was going to have to. After I took care of Valerie and the baby, after I checked on Isaac, after I talked to Raven. "What time does Willemina want me to come over tomorrow?" I asked.

Ariana asked Willi then relayed the message. "She said she'll make lunch. Twelve-fifteen. Raven works until two in the morning. She'll be up by then."

I nodded.

"Willi says don't forget the benefit photos."

~~~

After I dropped Ariana off at her house, I picked up the pictures and drove home. When I pulled into the yard, Thurman came around the corner of the house leading Blue. Valerie sat atop the horse holding Cody in front of her with one hand as she grasped the saddlehorn with the other. Everyone but Blue looked as though they were having the time of their life. Blue has fun only when he's breaking into Mrs. Lyttle's garden, and he hadn't been able to do that since Thurman fixed the gate.

Valerie came in a few minutes after I entered the house and helped me cook supper. I let her do the talking. Thurman had shown her around the place while I was gone.
~~~

They fed the catfish in the stock pond, walked down the lane to watch "those sweet Sherman boys" playing in the yard (I didn't tell her "those sweet Sherman boys" swear like an R-rated movie when Thurman's not close enough to knock their heads together), and met Mrs. Lyttle who gave Thurman another bag of garden-fresh vegetables.

Over dinner, Thurman told me he and Valerie had a nice visit getting acquainted.

"Oh?" I said, the hairs on the back of my neck standing up. This attribute has nothing to do with extraordinary sensing ability. When the hairs on the back of my neck stand up, it has to do with nearly thirty years of espousal experience. I know my husband. He had found out something in his nice little visit with Valerie that was going to bite me in the behind later.

"Yep. Valerie told me what happened when Isaac was arrested. She told me where they lived, about her family, about how she's doing in school. We had a real nice visit." The calm, relaxed, nonchalant way Thurman said "a real nice visit" made me very uneasy.

After supper, my nervousness increased ten-fold. As Valerie loaded the dishwasher and I put away leftovers, Thurman received a phone call. I listened to Thurman's end of the conversation. "Can it wait 'til tomorrow?" ... "What about her?" This he asked as he looked straight at me. "Who is he?" ... "He'll be there when I get there?" When he hung up, he told me was going into town. His excuse was that Luis needed some help with a repair at his house. From the way he was looking at me, it was a pretty serious repair.

Of course, I might have been imagining that the "her" in "What about her?" was me. It's not that I was keeping anything from Thurman—not anything serious, like a physical assault—but I felt stupid enough knowing I shouldn't have put myself at risk in the first place without letting my husband know how stupid I was. And if he found out, he might do something even more stupid.

Quit being melodramatic, I told myself. Thurman has always been level-headed. Cool, calm, and collected. Like when Sam was four and tied a bath towel around his neck then climbed on top of the barn roof to fly away like Superman. Unfortunately, he didn't fly far. Fortunately, he landed in a pile of sawdust. Unfortunately, he still broke his arm and was gouged and pierced by large wood chips. I ran around the yard flapping my arms like a chicken being chased by a fox and screaming "My baby! My baby!" Thurman scooped Samuel up, ordered me and Marissa into the car and drove, without a word, to the hospital. Thurman remained composed in situations where most people would lose it. Heck, he hardly ever raised his voice. I was definitely overreacting to his reaction. Or rather, my image of his reaction.

I also didn't tell him I was looking into Claire's murder, because I didn't want him to tell me to mind my own business. And I hadn't told him about Ariana threatening to divorce Dawson even though they were his friends, too. But that was because if I said it aloud, it might make it true, and I didn't want that to happen.

It's not that I like keeping secrets from my husband; it just happens sometimes.

"Wait," I said, realizing now was the time to unload some of the burden. "I got the pictures from the benefit, don't you want to see them?"

"I'll see them later," he said as he hurried out the door.

"May I see them?" Valerie asked.

"Sure." I took the packages off the bar, and we sat at the kitchen table. I opened the first package, and we went through them one by one. Then Cody climbed into Valerie's lap. When Valerie wouldn't let him hold the photos, he decided it was time to act like a two-year-old. He pitched himself back and forth and screamed at the top of his lungs. Valerie tried distracting him with toys, then a cookie, but to no avail.

"I'm sorry," she said. "I'd like to see them, but I better get him ready for bed."

"It's all right," I said. "What time do you want me to get you up for school?"

"I don't want to go to school. I want to see Isaac."

"The police chief said Monday afternoon would be the earliest you could see him. Let me take you to school in the morning, and hopefully, we'll be able to see him after I pick you up at three-thirty. Okay?"

She considered it a moment then nodded.

"I'll wake you at six."

When she left the kitchen, I looked through the rest of the photos in the stack, but I wasn't really seeing them. Thoughts and emotions splashed around in my brain like flotsam and jetsam batted around by the tide. First, overwhelming guilt splashed up. Thurman was my husband. He had the right to know what had happened at Valerie's house. I shouldn't be keeping secrets from him. I should have told him the minute he walked in the door last night. Then anger crashed in and swept the guilt out to sea. I was so stupid. Stupid, stupid, stupid to put myself in that situation. Then righteous indignation and a deep hatred floated up next to anger. I had permission to be in Valerie's house. Her mother's boyfriend didn't. He had no right to be there. If it had been Valerie and the baby alone in the house when he arrived....

The trouble was, trying to bury trauma keeps the hounds of hell at bay for only a little while. Sooner or later, those dogs chew through their chains, and the next thing you know, you're staring into the jowls of acidic drool, putrid breath, and sharp, jagged teeth. The hounds created by suppressing what had happened the previous night were close to breaking out of the enclosure my mind had built.

I put away the photos, went into my office, and tried to work on the accounts. I didn't have much luck there either. My mind kept wandering back to the scene in Valerie's kitchen, replaying the attack over and over. I relived the fear I felt when Tony appeared in the doorway, the terror that filled me when he grabbed my arm, the disgust I felt when he pushed himself against me. The image of what would have happened if Jerome had not appeared when he did. I grabbed for the wastebasket and threw up.

I sat at the desk with my head on my arm for several minutes until I felt steady enough to go to the bathroom to wash my face and brush my teeth. I went back to the office, removed the plastic liner from the wastebasket, and dropped it in the trash can in the garage. I sprayed the room with air freshener, went back to the bathroom to shower and change into a clean nightgown, then put on my robe and went into the family room to watch television and wait for Thurman.

Chapter Nineteen

Keeping the secret from Thurman was almost as heavy a load to carry as the assault itself. I'd made up my mind to tell him everything as soon as he walked in the door.

The weather report on the ten o'clock news had just come on when I heard his truck pull up. I waited on the couch. The bruise on his chin and his skinned knuckles told me he'd done more than help Luis with a home repair. "What happened?" I asked.

His voice was tense. "You tell me."

At those words, the raw emotion I'd held in check for the last twenty-four hours exploded in a torrent of tears and uncontrollable sobs.

Thurman's voice shook as his own tears fell. "How could you put yourself in that position? Don't you know I can't live without you? What if he had killed you?"

"I know. I know," I sobbed. "I'm sorry. It's all my fault. I shouldn't have gone there at dark. I knew something was wrong. But I was already there, and the baby's medicine was in the house, and I was just going to run in and grab it and get back in the car and come home, and then he was in the kitchen, and I tried to fight him, and if Jerome hadn't come by when he did, I—"

Thurman sat beside me and pulled me into his arms. "Shhh. It's not your fault," he said. "It's not your fault."

The tears poured, my nose ran like a waterfall, and I sobbed so hard my ribs ached.

He held me until I stopped shaking. "When Jerome told me he went to Valerie's house, and you were there, and you were attacked by that sonovabitch, I wanted to kill him."

"Jerome?"

"Gardner."

"Is that his name?"

"Tony Gardner. That sonovabitch needed to be taught a lesson. He needed to be castrated."

I looked up at him, fearfully. "You didn't...."

"I wanted to, but Luis and Jerome wouldn't let me. Jerome—"

"Jerome castrated him?" I said alarmed, remembering the switchblade.

"No one castrated him. We're going to take care of Gardner tomorrow."

"What?"

He pulled away so he could see my face, and make sure I could see his. "I'm really angry with you, Darby."

"You just said it wasn't my fault."

"The attack on your life wasn't your fault. But you shouldn't have been there alone after dark. It scared the hell out of me when I found out. I can't live without you, damn it. I'm angry, because you should have told me. I shouldn't have had to find out through Luis."

I put two and two together. Jerome knew Luis through the school. He knew Luis worked for Thurman. And when

Luis heard what had happened, he called Thurman.

"Why didn't you tell me?" Thurman asked.

"I wanted to, but I was afraid you'd kill him and end up in jail beside Isaac. You're not going to kill him are you?"

"No. If I was going to kill him, I would have done it tonight. He deserves it. Tomorrow, we're going to the police station. You are going to press charges against that bastard."

~~~

Thurman was still angry with me when we went to bed. He turned away, leaving me to stare at his back. I knew the disappointment that I had kept things from him would melt away after a few days. But I fell asleep feeling very alone.

Sometime in the night, Thurman cooled off. He woke me with hugs and kisses. He had something more physical in mind, but that hope was dashed when we heard doors opening and closing across the hall. "We'll take this up later," he said as he rolled away and got out of bed.

~~~

I had some time before I was to meet him at the police station, so I walked with Valerie to her classroom after we dropped the baby off at the day care center. Some of the students were certain to know about Isaac's arrest by now. I noticed a few of the students staring at Valerie when we entered the room, but no one said anything to her.

After checking with Cindy Soto to see if it was a convenient time, I announced, "I brought the pictures to show you, Julian."

"I want to see 'em," another student shouted. "Me, too," echoed around the room.

"Everyone settle down," Cindy said, as her gaze swept the room. When the kids had quieted, she turned to me. "May we pass them around the classroom?"

"Sure. Everyone in here worked on the decorations. I'm sure they'd all like to see the fruits of their labor."

The students nodded.

Conveniently, the number of photo envelopes I held matched the number of tables around which the students sat. "I'll put a package at each table. I don't mind if you get the pictures in each stack out of order, but please keep the stack with the envelope they came in. And hold the pictures by the edges," I said, demonstrating.

I passed out the photos then sat at one of the tables with the students. Cindy sat at another table to look at the photos circulating there. The kids commented on the decorations, the tuxedos and evening gowns, the tables spilling over with food, and of course, the hospitality bars rimmed with liquor bottles.

The pictures had almost made the round of all the students when Trini, a freckle-faced blonde said, "Hey, look. There's Nathan." She leaned over to the girl next to her pointing to the photo in her hand. "You heard about his mom, didn't you?"

"She's dead," a boy across the room said.

"Yeah," another said. "It happened at the party. Somebody killed her."

"Isaac killed her," Trini said. Horrified, she looked at Valerie. The whole room turned to stare. Valerie's face clouded over. She stood, picked up her bookbag, and slipped it over one shoulder.

"Shut up, Trini," someone said.

"I'm sorry, Val." Trini shrugged. "It just slipped out."

I walked over to stand beside Val. "Isaac did not kill her," I said to the class.

"The cops arrested him."

"They're mistaken," I said. "Valerie, do you want to go?"

Leticia rose from her desk and came over to Valerie. "You don't have to go. Y'all quit picking on her."

"Valerie," Cindy said. "I understand why you would want to go home, but I want you to stay. It's going to be just as hard to face the questions tomorrow as it is today."

Valerie, still clutching the strap of the bookbag with both hands, looked at me.

"Mrs. Soto is right. Tomorrow or the next day or the next day. Sooner or later, you're going to have to talk about this with your classmates."

Valerie looked around the room. Several of the students said she didn't have to talk about it if she didn't want to.

"I want her to talk about it," Julian said.

"Julian," Cindy said, "it's not up to you. It's Valerie's decision."

"I heard Nathan's mom got what she asked for."

"No one deserves to get killed, Julian." Cindy turned to Valerie. "Valerie? Do you want to talk about it? I can ask the counselor to join us."

Valerie nodded. She set her bookbag on the floor and slid into her chair. "I'll be all right, Mrs. Matheson."

"Everyone, put the pictures back into the envelope, so I can collect them," Cindy said.

"We didn't get to see them all," Julian said.

"I'll bring them again," I said, walking over to Trini's table. "May I have that picture?"

She handed it to me. I didn't see Nathan at first. The photo showed a smiling couple holding up flutes of champagne in a toast. A waitperson, farther in the distance, offered the tray of champagne to a group of other guests. In the picture's background you could see the musicians' empty chairs set up in front of the Vienna backdrop. I handed the photo back to the girl. "Where is Nathan?" I asked.

"Right there," she said, pointing as she handed it back.

I took the photo. In the background, between the chairs and the backdrop, it appeared as if Nathan, dressed in black tie, was about to be trampled on by the rearing Lipizzan stallion.

Chapter Veinte

I circled the block and found a two-hour parking space under a large live oak right in front of the police station. I pulled up to the curb and parked. As I was getting out, Thurman pulled up across the street, and we walked into the police station together.

"If the chief's not busy, I'd like a word with him," Thurman said to the uniformed officer who came to the reception window.

Thurman stopped in regularly to shoot the breeze with Jim Swanson. It was obvious the officer knew Thurman from previous visits. He nodded, picked up the phone, and punched in an extension. "Chief, Mr. Matheson is here to see you." After a few more exchanges, the officer put down the phone and told us to "go on back. You know where his office is."

Thurman thanked him as he led me to the locked steel door that clicked open when we approached it. The door closed behind us, and Thurman held my hand as we walked around the corner and down the hall to the chief's office. I had been relatively relaxed when I'd first arrived, but with each step, I grew more nervous.

When we were seated, Jim asked, "What can I do for you?"

Thurman told him I was there to press assault charges against Tony Gardner.

"Were you hurt?" Jim's expression was serious.

I shook my head.

"What happened?"

I told him everything. Why I had been in Pleasant Valley in the first place all the way up to when one of my students showed up and saved me.

"Who was this student?"

"Why?" I didn't think Jerome would appreciate being questioned by the cops any more than Isaac did.

"Because he's a witness."

"He probably doesn't want to get involved."

"Why not?"

"I just think he wouldn't want to get involved."

"He's already involved. You need to tell me everything, Darby, or would you feel more comfortable talking to someone else?" He picked up the phone and punched in some numbers. "You need to talk to a detective anyway."

Thurman shook his head. "There's a little more to it than that."

Jim replaced the phone on its cradle. "Does the something have to do with the bruise on your face?"

"Yes," Thurman said. "And the bruises I put on Tony Gardner."

"Fill me in," Jim said.

"I kicked his ass."

Jim put his elbows on his desk and leaned forward. "I understand why you did it, but I wish you'd called me yesterday. We could have picked him up. Then there wouldn't be any repercussions against you."

"You going to arrest me?"

"Not unless I have to, and if this guy insists, I might have to."

"Bullshit."

"I agree, but that's how it works. What happened?"

I was really feeling rotten now. If I had called 9-1-1 or gone to the police station and called Thurman from there, Gardner would be in jail and my husband wouldn't be in any trouble. "It's my fault. I didn't tell Thurman when it happened. He had to find out from Luis."

"How did Luis know?" Jim asked.

"Jerome called him," Thurman said.

"Jerome who?"

"Jerome Steele. The guy who came to the rescue."

"I know Jerome Steele. He's one of the biggest dealers in this town."

Thurman's head snapped around and gave me a look that would freeze-dry boiling tar.

"I didn't know that," I said innocently.

His expression changed to an and-a-cow-doesn't-poop-in-the-pasture look.

"I've never seen Jerome selling drugs," I said.

"Darby," Thurman said ominously.

"I haven't. Besides, I might be dead if he hadn't come along when he did."

"Or raped," Thurman said. "I don't care what Jerome's day job is. He ran off Gardner and got Darby back to her car safely."

"How does Luis know Jerome?"

"Luis doesn't sell drugs, *or do drugs,*" I said. "He knows Jerome through the school. Jerome knows Luis works for Thurman. He worked with Luis on the art project we did this summer—the backdrops for the benefit."

"The same benefit where Claire Nathe was murdered,"

Jim said. "Thurman, in two days you've managed to find a body *and* assault someone. Do you think you could stay in your woodshop for a day or two? We have enough work around here."

"I'll see what I can do," he said sarcastically.

We sat in silence for a few moments, then the chief said, "Finish. Luis called you after Steele called him."

"Yep. Luis told me he needed to tell me something, but he didn't want to tell me over the phone. When I got to his house, Jerome was waiting. He told me what had happened. I insisted he tell me where I could find Gardner. Jerome made a few calls, found out he was at a bar. The Sunset. I got in my truck; Luis and Jerome jumped in. I told them I didn't need any help; but they weren't coming along to help—they were coming along to keep me from killing him."

"What kind of shape are we going to find this guy in?"

"I only got in one good punch before they pulled me off of him."

"One?" the chief asked skeptically.

"Maybe two. He was an arrogant sonovabitch. He had the nerve to say Darby came on to him."

I could feel the blood drained from by face. "You don't believe that?"

"No. Hell, no!" He reached for my hand.

Jim sat quietly for a moment, then said, "I want you to look through some mug shots."

"You can pick him up at Valerie's mother's house." I gave him the address. "He's the reason she's staying with us. I didn't want her left alone in the house, in case...."

"In case Gardner came looking for her," Jim said.

I nodded.

"Then why did you go there alone?" my husband asked like I was the biggest moron in the world.

"I didn't know he was going to walk in the house," I said angrily. "I'm the victim here!"

"*I know.* That's what's making me crazy," he shot back. "That sonovabitch had no right.... I can't stop imagining what he might have done, and I can't help wishing you had stayed home instead of going to Pleasant Valley in the first place."

"Me either!" I yelled, snatching my hand away and jumping up. "If I *had* been raped, I sure as hell wouldn't rely on you for sympathy." I turned to the chief, still shouting. *"Where are the damn mug shots?"*

Chapter Twenty-one

I was mad at Thurman, he was mad at me, and Jim was smart enough to assign different officers to each of us. I told my story to Officer Tracy Williams, a soft-spoken female detective dressed in a tropical print shirt and khaki slacks. She pulled up computer file mug shots, and I searched until I located Gardner, which didn't take long. He was in the files, which meant he had a record.

Thurman didn't stop off to say "bye," "see you later," or "kiss my butt" when his interview was over which was just *fine* with me. But when Officer Williams escorted me to the front lobby, I peered through the glass door to see that Thurman's truck was gone, and that pissed me off but good. If he wanted to go back to giving me the silent treatment, I could give as good as I got.

With Tony Gardner identified, I had more important things to do anyway. I asked to see the chief again.

"For a school marm, you keep some pretty shady company," he said when I entered his office.

"Are you referring to my husband as a shady character?" I sat in the chair he offered then waited until he sat.

"I'm referring to Jerome Steele and Isaac Molina."

"They're not shady characters. They're kids."

"Not legally. If indicted they're both old enough to be charged as adults. If Molina is found guilty, he could end up on death row."

"He's not going to be found guilty," I said. I opened my purse and removed a photo. "Here." I leaned forward and placed it on his desk.

"What's this?" he asked, reaching for it.

"Proof that Nathan Nathe was at the benefit."

"So?"

"So. He had opportunity to kill his mother." I didn't necessarily believe Nathan killed Claire. I'd only begun to entertain the idea when Trini pointed him out. However, it was a possibility, and I wanted to get the chief thinking that the killer could be someone other than Isaac.

Jim looked at the snapshot. "All I see is the kid was at the benefit. This picture doesn't show him killing his mother."

"But he was angry with her for dictating which college he would attend."

"That's not much motive. And it's not proof. There were a lot of people in attendance, including Isaac Molina. Plus, we have a belt with Molina's finger prints and witnesses that heard him threaten her. There is no evidence against the son." His look was patronizing. "But you can keep trying."

Defeated, I reached for the photo.

He shook his head. "I'll keep it." He held it by the edges and fanned it back and forth. "This one's not the only picture taken that night. Where are the rest?"

I handed over all the envelopes.

"And the negatives?"

"They're in there." I slouched back in my chair. "Why do you need them when you've already charged Isaac?"

"There's no such thing as too much evidence."

I hoped if there was nothing in the photos to implicate Nathan, there would be nothing to further implicate Isaac. "When can I see him?" I asked.

Jim picked up his phone and punched in an extension. "Brad, what's the status on Isaac Molina?" He listened for a moment then said, "thanks," and hung up. "Your boy is being arraigned as we speak. You can see him this afternoon. Anything else I can do for you?"

I shook my head, thanked him, and left.

I was on my way to Willemina's when my cell phone rang. I turned onto a side street and parked at the curb. By the time I was able to retrieve the phone from the bottom of my purse, it had stopped ringing, but the LED read Wu, D. I pressed "call" and he answered on the second ring.

"Hi, Dawson," I said.

"What is wrong with Ariana?" He sounded frustrated and upset.

"What do you mean?" I asked.

"She accused me of having an affair when I walked in the door this morning, then asked me if I wanted a divorce. I thought she'd been on edge because she was spreading herself too thin. I thought she'd calm down after the benefit. Where did she get such a ridiculous idea?"

"She didn't tell you?"

"She left."

"Left?"

"She said she was going to the Houston store. But she won't answer her cell phone. What's with her?"

"Do I have to get in the middle of this?" I asked.

"Don't play innocent. You spent half the day with her yesterday. You know what's bothering her. Cough it up."

Ariana's going to kill me for opening my mouth, I thought, *but if I tell Dawson, he'll prove that he's faithful, they'll make up, and everyone will live happily ever after.* So I quickly said, "Lily."

"Lily? What's Lily got to do with this?"

His puzzled tone of voice gave me hope. "Lily's who you're having the affair with. *Isn't she?*"

There was a protracted silence from Dawson's end. "How did she find out?" The frustration had left his voice, and it was replaced with a mildly humorous tone.

I stammered a bit before blurting out, "She listened to your messages."

"She listened to a message left for *me* by Lily on *my* recorder?" His voice was growing increasingly jovial. "What did the message say?"

"It's not funny Dawson. Here I am, taking your side in this mess, and you're amused? I thought you had more respect for Ariana."

He was laughing now. "I have the utmost respect for my wife. I thought she respected me. I didn't know she was listening to my private phone messages."

"She wouldn't have if she hadn't found the check for the apartment."

"*And* going through my canceled checks? Hmmm. What did the message say?"

"Haven't you listened to your messages?"

Dawson said nothing.

"It was something about bow may. I don't know. I forgot how to say it." I was growing perturbed.

"Biao mei," he corrected.

"Yes," I said. "*Biao mei.* Girlfriend."

"Biao mei Lily," he said.

"I *knew* you listened to it. How could you do this to Ariana?"

"Ariana doesn't speak Mandarin. How did she find out *biao mei* meant girlfriend?"

"She called your mother."
"My mother?" He chuckled.
"Why are you laughing?"
"Because it's funny."

Chapter Twenty-two

Funny? I didn't think it was so damn funny. Between dealing with my own jackass of a husband and Ariana's jackass, I was in a rotten mood by the time I got to Willi's.

"Has Ariana talked to you about Dawson?" I asked her as she let me in. I was prepared for her to say "no."

So I was taken aback when she said, "About his cheating? I told her men weren't saints." She turned and led the way to the kitchen.

"Thurman's a saint. Richard's a saint," I said, "isn't he?"

She waved me to a seat at the breakfast bar, which ran the length of the counter between the breakfast room and kitchen. Willi walked into the kitchen and stood at the counter opposite me. "He is now, but he wasn't always."

"You're kidding!"

She picked up a glass and dropped ice into it, poured ice tea from a pitcher, then set the glass in front of me. "I wish I was, but I'm not."

"Not Richard."

"It was a long time ago, and I'd rather not discuss it."

"Did you tell Ariana?"

"I didn't go into the details, but I told her a man could do worse things than stray."

"You're sure forgiving," I said, "I don't know if I could forgive Thurman." I really didn't know if I could forgive him if he slept with another woman. I hoped I'd never have to find out.

"Like I said, it was a long time ago, before I was pregnant with Roslyn. We were both young. In the early years of our marriage, we both made mistakes."

"You had an affair!"

"Revenge is not always sweet. The point is, Ariana has to decide for herself what she's going to do about her marriage."

So did Willi or didn't she? I guess I wasn't going to find out. "Ariana asked Dawson for a divorce," I said.

"She told you that?"

"He told me."

"How did he take it?"

"When he hung up from talking to me, he was laughing."

"*Laughing?* He doesn't sound too broken-up. Or was it a hysterical laugh, like he'd just gone insane?"

"He sounded insane to me. Everything he said sounded like he was admitting to an affair. But his manner sure wasn't one of guilt." I tried to recall if I'd felt *bug guts.* No. Not even a tinge. I'd just felt mad. "It was the weirdest conversation I've had in a while."

Willemina put her finger to her lips. "Shhh."

I listened. Footsteps sounded in the hall.

Raven appeared dressed in shorts so short they were barely visible beneath her oversized paint-splattered shirt. Her hair was pulled back in a circular comb that pulled the hair tight to the scalp near her face, but made it spring out like the crown of a kingfisher in the back. She wore no makeup, but given her gene pool, it wasn't needed. She had her mother's facial features and her father's height and ebony skin tone.

"Hi, Darby." She walked over and reached for a hug.

I held her at arm's length, giving her shirt a questioning look.

Puzzled, she looked at the front of her shirt. "It's dry," she said. "I haven't started painting today." She hugged me, looked at my shirt as she stepped back, and gasped.

I gasped too, looking down quickly.

She giggled. "Just kidding."

"Smart aleck," I said, wiping at the nonexistent paint.

Raven walked over to Willi. "What were you talking about?" she asked, looking into the pot Willi was stirring.

"Nothing," her mother said.

She looked from her mother to me suspiciously. "You just don't want me to know."

I gave her my village idiot smile.

"Don't tell me. I don't care." She turned back to Willi. "Is lunch ready?"

"Almost."

"What are you painting?" I asked.

"You've *got* to see this," Willi said, putting down the spoon she held and wiping her hands on a tea towel. "Follow me."

Raven blocked her way. "Mom. I'm not finished."

"You've finished the utility room." Willi put her hands on Raven's shoulder and twisted her around.

"All right. Just keep in mind I still have more to do."

"I will," I said.

I followed them through the family room to the far end of the house and into the utility room. The washer, dryer, and freezer were gone. The walls had been stripped of the original wall paper—a brown, black and gold print that Willi had settled on but never liked, saying it reminded her of Richard's boxer shorts. A wash, starting at the ceiling and fading from soft yellow to orange to straw, covered all four walls giving the effect of the African savanna. Around the four walls, Raven had painted a clothes line stretched between acacia and palm trees. From the line hung pants, shirts, dresses, underwear, and other laundry. An African elephant was apparently removing clothes from the line. A green print dress dangled by one clothes pin with the other clasped neatly in the determined elephant's trunk. A giraffe, with legs spread to get his head under a hanging sheet, seemed to be looking at me with crossed eyes. A baboon pulled a red shirt out of a laundry basket, two hyenas played tug of war with a towel, and a zebra drank from the wash tub while another blew bubbles as if he had already made that mistake. Numerous other African animals were having a grand time. In the background, an African woman waving her arms was running from her hut toward the chaos the animals were making of her laundry. Raven had painted the mural so it could be viewed once all the appliances were back in place.

"Wow," I said.

"Do you like it?"

"Wow! I am so impressed." I looked around the room. "What do you have to finish? It looks done to me."

"A few touches here and there. And the powder room," she said, pointing toward the half-bath.

I walked into the room that was stripped to the Sheetrock. "What are you going to paint in here?"

"Same theme, different location," she said.

I imagined the elephant sitting on a toilet reading the newspaper. "Call me when you're finish. I want to see it."

When we returned to the kitchen, Willi invited us to sit in the dining room, which I call the Ming Dynasty room because of the oriental decor. Lunch at Willemina's was an *occasion.* The place mats were ivory linen. Jade napkin rings encircled matching napkins which held silver. Not stainless.

Silver. At my house you'd be lucky to get plastic.

The first course was an aromatic seafood bisque. When I commented on how delicious it was, she said, "I'll give you the recipe. I got it from the chef at the Half Moon in Jamaica."

"Thanks. I'll add it to your recipe for peach buns."

She frowned, remembering our conversation of two days earlier. "Never mind. I'll save my recipe cards."

"You don't cook?" Raven asked.

"Every day," I said. "But if I'm following a recipe, it's on the back of the box."

"I feel the same way. Good thing Mom likes to cook, or Daddy and I would live off pizza and fast food."

"If you're ever going to get married, you better learn to enjoy cooking," Willi said.

"Who says I'm getting married?"

"James isn't going to wait forever."

"If James and I get married, he can cook."

"Are you going to get married?" I asked.

She squished her brows together in an *are-you-crazy?* look.

"I'd love to plan another wedding like Roslyn's, but Raven keeps putting James off," Willi said.

"That's just what I want. A big spectacle with gaudy bridesmaid dresses, groomsmen who look like undertakers, and a wedding cake as big as this room. No, thanks."

Perturbed, Willi said, "Roslyn's wedding was beautiful. And she and Curtis are very happy together."

"That's another thing. It all ends with James and me building a nest of domesticity like Roslyn and Curtis. God forbid!"

"My daughter, the bohemian." Willi rose and noisily cleared away the empty bowls.

"I'm sorry to disappoint you, Mom. If I get married, I'm eloping."

"You are *not* eloping."

"You have two more daughters. Rickie and Rianna will be happy to let you do the wedding planner thing for their weddings."

"Thank goodness!"

"Can we change the subject, now?"

"Please change it," Willi said. She spun away and stalked out of the dining room.

Raven grinned devilishly.

"You're just needling your mom aren't you?"

"Yeah," she whispered, "but don't tell her."

Willi walked back into the dining room carrying a tray. She set a plate of salad greens in front of me then plopped Raven's in front of her with an angry glare.

Raven smiled sweetly at her mother. "Thank you, Mommy."

"Don't 'mommy' me," Willemina said as she took her seat.

Raven turned to me, her eyes twinkling. She ate a bite of her salad, then said, "You wanted to know about Kamie Nathe?"

"Claire's daughter? Yes, please. She graduated with you?"

"Uh huh. What do you want to know?"

"Whatever you can tell me."

"Hang on." She got up and left the room. In a few moments she returned with a blue and gold book and set it on the table. "My yearbook."

She flipped through a few pages then turned it around and pushed it toward me, pointing to a photo on one of the pages. "That's Kamie."

"She resembles her dad," I said. The caption beneath her picture read, *Kamie Claire Nathe.*

Raven pulled the book away, flipped to a back page, then slid the book to me, again pointing to a place on the page.

I read: *NATHE, KAMIE—Cheerleader 2,3,4; FBLA 1,2,3,4; Pep Club 1,2,3,4; Spanish Club 3,4.*

"She was active in extracurricular activities," I said. "Was she as good a student as her brother?"

"I don't know her brother. I guess she was a good student. You had to keep a good grade point average to stay in sports and clubs. I know she was real social. She ran with the popular kids."

"That's the opposite of Nathan. When I met him, he seemed very shy. Jaclyn said that he was sweet, didn't talk much, and he was afraid of his mother. She said she thought Gary was afraid of Claire, too. I wonder if Kamie was afraid of Claire."

"Kamie wasn't afraid of anything."

"What do you mean?"

"Well, I wouldn't call her a bully, but you didn't want to cross her. She could cut you to ribbons verbally."

"Does she still live in Dulcinea?"

"I don't think so, but I lost track of a lot of people after we graduated. Patrick Koontz was her boyfriend. He has the early morning show on KDTX. He might know."

Chapter Twenty-three

We finished our salad as Raven talked about the other project she was working on, a mural for the visitors' center at one of the plants, also a wildlife theme. Nature-and-petroleum-co-existing propaganda, Raven called it, but the conservationist in her didn't object to the point that she'd turn down the money.

Willi served the main course of broiled snapper with a light lemon butter sauce, rice, and broccoli florets with baby carrots.

It was after this course, the conversation slowed allowing the Tony Gardner nightmare to crash through the protective barrier I'd built.

I told them I'd been attacked. I said it so matter-of-factly, they both looked at me like I was talking about the weather; that is, until the dam broke.

Willi reached over and held my hand. "Darby, are you all right? What happened?"

"Oh my gosh, Darby," Raven said. "Were you hurt?"

I told them what had taken me to Valerie's house, about Tony appearing in the door as I was leaving, and about Jerome showing up like a guardian Hell's Angel. "This is really getting old," I said, using my napkin to dry my face. "I'm going to quit thinking about it," I sniffed. "I bawl like a lost calf every time I do."

"Of course, you do," Willi said.

"If Thurman wasn't being such an ass, it wouldn't be so bad," I said. "Gardner told Thurman, just before Thurman mopped up the ground with him, that *I* had come on to *him*. And I'm beginning to think Thurman believes that."

"He doesn't believe it, honey. He's smarter than that. He's just upset that he wasn't there to protect you."

"He's acting like Cro-Magnon man. Like *he* was victimized instead of me."

"He was, sweetie. You're a part of him," Willie said.

"Thurman beat him up?" Raven asked.

I told them about our conversation with Chief Swanson, giving statements to the officers, and identifying Gardner on the computer.

"Good. They'll put him behind bars, and he won't be able to hurt anyone else," Willi said.

I started bawling again. He *had* hurt me. Not physically, but he'd shattered my security. I'd never feel completely safe again. "Thurman wanted to castrate him, but Luis and Jerome wouldn't let him."

"They should have," Raven said vehemently.

Willi nodded in agreement. She released my hand long enough to let me blow my nose on her fine linen napkin.

Then I cried even harder. "I ruined your linen."

"It will wash." She patted me on the arm. "I know what you need."

She disappeared into the kitchen and returned with coffee and dessert. Crème brûlée. My favorite.

"You're such a good friend," I sputtered.

"Now you stop crying," she said. "Salty tears don't go well with crème brûlée."

She was right. I excused myself and went to the bathroom to calm down and wash my face. When I got back to the table, I sat back and sipped on my coffee.

After a few minutes, Willi deftly changed the subject. "Did you get the photos?"

I dove into the dessert. "Mmmm." It *was exactly* what I needed. "I picked them up yesterday and gave them to the chief this morning."

She looked panic stricken but was probably afraid I'd start crying again if she said what she was probably thinking. *You gave them to the chief? We'll never get them back.*

Her expression made me laugh. "I made double prints. They're in my purse."

Willi breathed a sigh of relief. "Thank goodness."

"Raven," I said, "would you mind getting them? They're in a brown sack with a rubber band around it in my purse. It's on the bar. Just dig around a while and you'll find it."

In a jiffy, she was back with the bag. I opened it and flipped through the snapshots until I found the one I was looking for. I handed it to Willi.

She scrutinized it a moment, then looked up. "I didn't know Nathan was at the event."

"I didn't either, until I saw that picture. Was he on the guest list?"

"No. Did he model?"

"No, there weren't that many men. I would have remembered."

"From how you described him earlier, he doesn't seem to be the modeling type," Raven said, reaching for the photo.

"He's an attractive boy."

"But you said he's shy."

I nodded. "Jaclyn Amayo's shy and she modeled."

I started to hand all the pictures to Willemina, but when she reached for them, I pulled the stack back and flipped through it again, not really knowing what I was looking for. I stopped at one of the first photos I had taken. It was of Gary taking a picture of a couple standing beside the Queen's guard. What was it about this picture? "Who are these people?" I showed it to Willi.

"Dean Moss and Sherilyn Rather."

"Do they know Claire?"

"I'll find out." She started to rise, but I motioned her to stay.

"Let's finish this marvelous lunch you fixed. We can do it later."

I returned to my dessert and was scraping the last molecule from the bottom of the glazed crock when she asked, "Do you want to go with me to the Nathe's? I made a casserole to take."

"I didn't know you made casseroles. I thought everything you cooked was gourmet."

"It's a gourmet casserole."

I looked at my watch. It was just one thirty. "As long as we're back here by three."

"You know this is a condolence call, but we may never have a better time to ask questions of the family. What do you think?"

"I think we'll never get a better chance to talk to the family," I said, pushing back from the table.

"Did you want to talk to Patrick Koontz?" Raven asked.

"Yes. But we can't do both this afternoon. Will you call him and see if we can meet tomorrow?"

"What time?"

I looked at Willi. "Nine or ten?"

"I have a meeting in the morning. The African American Chamber of Commerce is planning the Fall Awards Banquet. I have to be there. But I'll be free in the afternoon."

I turned back to Raven. "Find out from him what's convenient, and we'll play it by ear."

While she called Patrick, I helped Willemina clean up the kitchen, which didn't take long; Willi's one of those use-a-dish-wash-a-dish types.

Raven found out Patrick would be available at the radio station at nine in the morning. I'd have to question him alone.

Chapter Twenty-four

The Nathes' two-story Victorian sits at the end of a cul-de-sac in the Oakwood subdivision, another upscale neighborhood in Dulcinea. The homes in Oakwood are older. Trees have grown higher than the rooftops, and the rooftops look a bit worn but not bad enough to be replaced just yet. The houses themselves are kept painted or high-pressure washed and in good repair, and most of the lawns are well cared for, either by the owners or a lawn care service.

I'd asked Willi to swing by a bakery so I could pick up a pecan pie on the way over. We put on our expressions of sympathy, and Willi rang the doorbell. It was answered by a grey-haired lady about my height and maybe fifty pounds heavier. She wore a bright flowered sleeveless shirt which did nothing to distract from the loose, sun-damaged skin hanging from her thick, upper arms. The buttoned-down shirt hung over stretch pants that didn't quite match any of the colors in the shirt.

She looked from Willemina, to me, then to the dishes we carried. "Come on in," she said in a voice as bright and loud as her shirt.

As she turned to lead us into the house, Willi and I looked at each other with the same question. *Who was this spunky Wal-Mart greeter?*

The dining room and greatroom were separated only by an expanse of carpet. To the right, the large dining room table sat eight. It was of heavy oak with the legs on either end supported by a grill of half-inch square dowels. It had a cozy jail cell look. The matching chairs were the same. Ramrod straight chair backs with the same bars. To the left the greatroom was furnished in the same style. Jail bar grill armrest for the sofa, love seat, and two chairs; the black leather cushions didn't do too much to soften the effect.

The pricey yet harsh decor didn't account for the tightness in my chest. That was caused by something else. I tried to ignore it. "What style do you call this furniture?" I asked Willi.

"Turn of the century. It's quite attractive," she said.

The grey-haired lady turned around, looked at the furniture, and said, "Each to your own. I like the kind of furniture you can sink into." I thought of Valerie's legless couch.

The accessories and wall hangings were sparse but had that purchased-at-Pier One look. There was only one item reflecting a personal touch. The family portrait, which must have been taken this year or last, hung over the fireplace. Gary, Claire, and Nathan. Kamie wasn't in it, for whatever reason. There were no other photos on the walls, none on tables. The Nathe home had the warmth and lived-in feeling of a furniture showroom.

We were led into the kitchen where I expected to see something reflecting the life of a normal family, like a refrigerator covered in snapshots or awards. Surely with Nathan's scholastic record, he would have earned awards

Claire would be proud to display. If so, they weren't in the kitchen.

"Are you friends of Gary?" the woman asked, taking the casserole from Willemina and setting it on the counter. I wondered, as I placed the pie beside the casserole dish, why she hadn't said "friends of Claire" since Claire was the one who had died.

Willemina introduced us, adding, "We're friends of Gary *and* Claire."

"You're probably not Claire's friends. You're just being polite. And I appreciate that. After all, a mother would like to think her daughter had lots of friends."

"You're Claire's mother?" Willemina asked, surprised.

"I'm Mildred Prasek. I'm her mother, believe it or not." She walked toward us as if to shake hands, but instead, she pushed between the two of us, opened a cabinet door and pulled out three coffee cups. "I don't know how she could have any friends," she continued. "Not real friends. She didn't have any growing up. I know that." She looked at me. "Oh, don't look so surprised. I'm her mother, and I loved her, but she wasn't a nice person." She walked over to the coffee pot and filled each cup. "How is it you know Claire?" she asked Willemina.

"Claire helped with several fund-raising events in the community. I became acquainted with her through them. And of course, we've used Gary's studio many times over the years for family portraits."

I felt I was the next to the last contestant in a spelling bee when Mildred asked me the same question. "I knew her through the charity functions," I said. BBLLLAAAP! The wrong answer buzzer went off in my head.

"So you *weren't* friends." She invited us to doctor our coffees then led us to the kitchen table. "Claire never did anything unless there was something in it for her." She didn't say it with malice, more like resignation.

How well you knew her, I thought, but I didn't say it out loud. It's perfectly all right for me to complain about my kids, but let someone else do it, and they're asking for a fight. I figured that was how Mildred felt. If I agreed with her, she might not take it well.

I knew Willemina had read her the same way when she said, "Claire was always very helpful."

Liar.

Mildred's spunk began to recede. "It's nice of you to say. I always hoped she'd change. We were never good enough for Claire. You know, she was telling everybody that Nathan was following in his grandfather's footsteps by going to Harvard." She laughed. "Harvard."

"Nathan's not going to Harvard?" I asked.

"Nathan's a smart boy. He's going to college. But he ain't followin' in anyone's footsteps. 'Specially not my Bernie. Bernie didn't finish high school. But he was a good man, God rest his soul. He passed away a few years back. He quit school in the eighth grade to help provide for the family after his daddy run off. Bernie was a yard man. He could teach the man who mows this yard a thing or two. And he always made sure we had a roof over our heads, and the kids had clothes on their backs and food on the table. But Claire was 'shamed of us. Good wasn't good enough. She always wanted more. Yep. Designer clothes, the latest this, the latest that—that's what was important to Claire."

We heard a door close down the hall. And presently, Nathan appeared behind us. He was dressed in starched khakis and a Polo shirt. Mildred rose from the table and walked around to put her arm around him. "These nice ladies came to pay their respects, sugar."

He looked uncomfortable until Mildred stepped away.

"Come on and sit down, and I'll cut some of that pie they brought."

"No, thanks. Are Dad and Kamie home yet?"

"Not yet. I guess they're still at the funeral home."

That answered a lot of questions. We never got around to asking for Gary, because Mildred couldn't quit talking about Claire.

Nathan looked lost—like a stranger in his own house.

"Nathan," I said, "come sit down and visit for a minute." I was getting an earful about Claire from her mother, but I still wanted to hear from Nathan.

He pulled out a chair from the end of the table and sat in it like he would flee if he had half a chance.

"We want to tell you how very sorry we are about your mother," I said.

"Thanks."

Willi reached over and patted his hands which he rested on the table in a double-fisted grip.

He looked at Willi. "Dr. Henry found my mom?"

She nodded. "He and Mr. Matheson," she said, nodding my way.

He glanced at me, then back at Willi. "I guess there wasn't anything they could do."

She shook her head.

We sat in silence a while, which was surprising. I expected Mildred to continue carrying the conversation, but she walked back into the kitchen and began cutting the pie that Nathan said he didn't want.

"Kamie's your sister?" I asked, trying to get a conversation going.

He nodded.

"Is she older than you?"

"She's twenty-three."

"Where does she live?"

He looked at me like I was prying, which I was.

"I noticed the family portrait in the living room and guessed she wasn't living here."

"She doesn't."

I might well have been back in the library trying to reel in the right information from a student. "I need a book," he'd say, tugging on my line. "What kind of book?" I'd ask, making one spin of the reel. "I don't know," he'd say, fighting at the end of the hook. "What subject are you working on?" I'd ask, letting him run for a bit. "History," he'd say. Sometimes this fishing trip took a while, but usually I was able to sink the hook, reel him in, net him, dress him and send him back to class, fried and with a side of baked beans. I was afraid Nathan was going to be the one that got away.

"I have a daughter who's twenty-three," Willie said, picking up where I had failed. "Do you know Raven?"

He shook his head.

"Maybe you know Rianna. She graduated last year. She's pre-med at Baylor."

"I remember her. She was in my calc class."

"Calculus? She took that in her senior year. You took calculus as a sophomore?"

"I like math."

It was no wonder the kid earned a scholarship. "Is that what you're going to major in? Math?" I asked.

"That's what I want to do."

"You must have done very well in high school to earn a scholarship to Harvard."

"You'd think he's still studying, with the amount of time he spends in his room," Mildred said, returning with a tray loaded with plates of pie, forks, and napkins. "I guess it's his way of mourning his loss," she said as if Nathan wasn't there. "Kamie's holding up better. But she's a tough kid. This is the first time I've spent any time with Nathan since he was young, what with circumstances the way they were between us and Claire. He's not as strong as his sister. That's why I told Gary I'd stay here with Nathan while he and Kamie made the arrangements. The coroner sent Claire's body to the funeral home yesterday. Nathan didn't want to go."

Nathan didn't seem to be all that eager to spend time with his grandmother, either. And who could blame him? His mother had just been killed, and his maternal grandmother seemed untouched by the event. But maybe that was *her* way of mourning her loss.

"Do you see Kamie often?" Willemina asked Mildred.

"Oh, sure. She's my boss." She giggled. "I would love to have seen Claire's face when she found out Kamie was slingin' hash. That's what Claire said—no daughter of hers was going to sling hash for a living. Kamie and Nathan use to come visit when they were little, and I'd take them to work with me at the Pancake House. But when Kamie told her mom she wanted to work in a restaurant when she grew up, Claire wouldn't let 'em come visit anymore. She wouldn't let us come see the kids. She didn't want our white-trash ways to rub off on them."

"She didn't let you visit the children?" Willi said. "How horrible."

"It near about killed us. But when Kamie was old enough to drive, she'd come see us once in a while. She'd tell Claire she was going somewhere else, then she'd come see us. As long as she made it back by her curfew, there wasn't any problem."

"Excuse me." Nathan stood up abruptly. "I'll be in my room."

"You didn't eat your pie," Mildred said.

"I don't want any."

As he turned to leave, I said, "You were at the benefit, Nathan. I have a snapshot."

He turned back to me, but took a few seconds to reply. "I took some equipment to my dad."

"You got all dressed up just to drop off equipment?"

I felt the blood leave my face, and I fought back the bile that was rising in my throat.

"Of course. It was formal." He turned away again and walked out.

"Nathan doesn't want to hear anything bad said against Claire, and that's understandable," Mildred said, seeming not to notice any difference in me. "But the truth's the truth."

Willi *had* noticed. "Are you all right? You look like you're coming down with the flu."

Trying to cover, I flew into a fake coughing fit. "I'm fine. Pie went down wrong."

She stared at me for a few more moments, as if waiting to make sure she wouldn't have to do the Heimlich maneuver on me. Presently, she turned back to Mildred. "How did Kamie become your boss?"

"She applied for the job."

"I mean—"

"Just joshin'. I know what you mean. You want the long story." She rose. "Let me get y'all some more coffee." She walked into the kitchen to retrieve the carafe. "Well, it was right after she graduated. We got a graduation announcement from her. Nathan didn't send one this year, but Kamie hand-delivered hers. Course Kamie was close to us and Nathan wasn't."

Mildred came back and poured coffee in each of our cups then stood at the table and talked. "That's why she left home. Claire found out Kamie came to see us, and something happened. Kamie never did tell us what, but it must have been real bad to make her leave. We know Claire took her car away from her even though Kamie had used her own money to buy it. She took the bus to Pasadena."

"You don't think taking her car away would make Kamie mad enough to run away?"

"No. It was something she won't talk about."

"She moved in with you?"

"We didn't know until about a year later that she was in Pasadena. She was afraid Claire would find her there, so she moved into a shelter for a few days, got a waitressin' job, and found a place to live for real cheap.

Claire would have found her at our place. Claire called us that very night. Then she started calling us more and more every day. It started out two and three times then went to eight and nine times a day. After a few weeks, she was calling then hanging up at all hours of the day and night. We had our phone number changed, then she showed up at the house. We let her walk all through it to see that Kamie wasn't there, that she hadn't been there. It seemed to satisfy her, at least she said she believed us, but then the letters started. Hateful, hateful letters. She wouldn't believe that we didn't know where Kamie was."

"How heartbreaking for you," Willi said.

"Yep." She nodded, turning to take the carafe back into the kitchen. She returned to her chair. "We called Gary and talked to him. We told him we didn't know where Kamie was and could he please get Claire to understand. He said he'd try. He must have gotten through to her. She finally stopped sending the letters."

I repeated Willi's question. "How *did* Kamie become your boss?"

Mildred's face lit up. "She finally came to see us. She'd been waitressin' and going to school. There's a hotel and restaurant school at the University of Houston. Kamie knew what she wanted, and she just kept working toward it. She manages the Garden Inn out by the airport. She hired me. I work in the lobby cafe at breakfast and lunch and sometimes at night if they're short-handed."

The doorbell rang, and Mildred hustled away to the front door.

"Why didn't they call the police when Claire started harassing them?" I whispered.

"Could you call the police on your child?"

"My kids would never treat me like that."

"I wonder if Claire called the police to report Kamie missing?"

"Don't you imagine she'd tell them Kamie ran away to her grandparents?"

"Maybe she didn't report Kamie missing because she didn't want anyone in Dulcinea to know her father was a yard man and her mother a waitress," Willi said.

"How could she let that get in the way of her daughter's safety?"

"Mildred said that something bad happened to Kamie. If Claire's mother would talk about her like that, imagine what Gary's parents would have to say," Willemina said.

"We could make a condolence call on them," I suggested. "Maybe they know what happened."

Willi pointed to her watch.

Valerie! It was almost time to pick her up. "I guess we better make it tomorrow."

Willemina and I took our coffee cups to the kitchen and placed them in the sink, gathered up our handbags and started into the living room where Mildred stood talking to a woman in her early twenties and a man in his thirties.

"I'm going to find the bathroom," I whispered. I detoured to the door in which Nathan had disappeared, knocked lightly and opened it a few inches.

He was lying on the bed reading, but sat up when I opened the door. The bed was spread in a brown and beige cover which matched the drapes. A computer desk sat in one corner. Books stood in neat rows in the bookcase. Framed certificates hung on the walls in neat, orderly groups.

I walked in and took a closer look. Achievement in Mathematics, Achievement in Science, Perfect Attendance, Outstanding Performance—NASA Space Camp, among others. "I was wondering where these were hiding."

He moved over and sat on the edge of the bed.

"Why did you wear your tuxedo to the benefit?" I asked.

"I told you. I had to drop off equipment for my dad."

"What did you have to drop off?"

"A light meter and a lens."

"But why the tux? If you were just dropping off a light meter and a lens, why did you have to get dressed up? Or why didn't you just wear a suit?"

He stood up, dropping the book on the bed. "What does it matter?"

I didn't know why it mattered. It just seemed so ... not like the typical teenager. "Just answer me. Did you put on the tuxedo so you would blend in?"

"Of course I wanted to blend in."

"So you could kill your mother?"

It was as though I'd slapped him. He actually flinched. "Why are you doing this? I didn't kill my mother. Isaac Molina killed her."

"No, Nathan. Isaac didn't kill her. Isaac didn't put on a tuxedo just to blend in, but *you did.*"

He started to cry. "I didn't want to embarrass her, so I dressed up. Where's the crime in that?"

"Were you angry at your mother for making you go to Harvard?"

"What?"

"You wanted to go to MIT."

"How do you know what I wanted?"

"I've been talking to people who know you. Who know your mother. Why was she forcing you to go to Harvard?"

"She wasn't forcing me. I wanted to go."

I pointed to the book on his bed. "Then why are you reading a course guide from MIT?"

Chapter Twenty-five

I was sick when we got in the car, but it wasn't *bug guts*. I was disgusted with myself. The only time I'd ever lit into a student like I lit into Nathan was when another kid's Game Boy had disappeared out of my desk. I'd felt like crap then, too. "Is this how police work works?" I asked, as we were driving out of Oakwood.

"What do you mean?"

"I don't think I'm cut out for it. I thought Nathan was lying, so I went back to talk to him. I wasn't very nice."

"I'm surprised you had it in you. You're too soft-hearted sometimes. Maybe we should reconsider and attend a few criminal justice classes at the college," she said prudently. "It might toughen you up."

"I'm going to have to get tough on my own. Isaac is sitting in jail. Can you imagine being behind bars for even an hour? He's been there since early Saturday morning. I'm not looking forward to facing him this afternoon."

"You didn't put him there."

"I know that, but I feel responsible for getting him out."

"He *did* assault a police officer," she reminded me.

"It wasn't his fault. He was provoked."

"You're sure about that?"

"No," I admitted. "He has a temper. And I wasn't there to see what happened. He *might* deserve being charged for assault but not *murder*."

We drove in silence for a while, then Willi said, "Claire behaved like an absolute beast toward her parents, didn't she?"

"Awful. You know, so far, we're getting a pretty grim picture of her. According to Jaclyn, Claire planted drugs in her desk then forced her to quit her job. Nathan was attending Harvard instead of MIT to keep Claire happy—and why she wasn't thrilled for him to attend the Massachusetts *flippen* Institute of Technology is beyond me. She refused to let her children visit *her own parents* then harassed them when Kamie ran away. I told Chief Swanson that Nathan had reason to kill his mom because she was forcing him to go to the college of *her* choosing."

"What did he say?"

"He said it was a pretty lame motive."

"It is."

"Yeah. I know. And Nathan didn't admit to it." I watched the stores and fast food restaurants move past the window. "Somebody killed her," I said.

"Too bad you don't have ESP," Willi said, taking her eyes off the road and giving me a hard look.

I felt myself blush. "If I did, it wouldn't work when I needed it to," I said wearily.

"How did you know they'd found Claire's body?"

I didn't like where this line of questioning was going and said nothing.

"The night she was killed, you said, 'They found her.'"

"I saw Thurman coming in the door to talk to Gary."

"No, you didn't. Thurman came in after you said it."

"It was a lucky guess."

"Hmmm. Well, of all the people we've talked to, who do you *guess* we should talk to next?"

I thought about it a minute. There was something wrong in the Nathe house, and it was wrong long before Claire was killed. "Patrick Koontz," I said.

"Why?"

"Because he knows why Kamie left home."

~~~

I picked up Valerie and Cody at three-fifteen. It took only ten minutes to get to the jail which was housed at the Sheriff's department. We were directed to the visitors' entrance where we were informed that only two visitors were allowed each day. I wanted to talk to Isaac. I wanted to ask him face-to-face about his arrest, about whether or not he'd seen Claire Nathe that evening, if he was holding up all right. But even though Cody was still a babe-in-arms, he counted as one of the two visitors. I felt it was more important for Isaac to see his son, so I told Valerie I would wait for her. She was allowed an hour.

I walked outside and called Ariana.

"I just got off the phone with Willemina," she said. "Why didn't you tell me about that son of a bitch?"

My thoughts went to Dawson, since he was the one she'd been calling names. "He's not really a son of a bitch," I said.

"*¿Que?* He attacked you! Willi said you couldn't quit crying when you were telling her about it."

"Oh," I said. "I thought you were talking about someone else."

"Well. It seems you've gotten over it."

I hadn't gotten over it. I didn't want to think about it. "I don't want to talk about it right now." I told her I was waiting for Valerie, that I wasn't going to get to talk to
~~~

Isaac, and that we had taken food to the Nathes. "Willi and I learned a lot about Claire from her mother."

"She told me. She also said she was concerned about you. She said you looked as if you were coming down with the flu. That bastard didn't rape you?"

"No. Please, let's talk about it later." I didn't want to start crying again.

She was quiet for a moment, then said, "In that case, if you were looking sick, it must have been *bug guts*."

"It was. Willi told you all about Claire harassing her parents?"

"Yes."

"And we already know what she did to Jaclyn."

"Yes. If you want to find out some more dirt, call Julia Thompson. She owns Lone Star Communications." She gave me the number, then explained. "I contacted my interior decorator. She belongs to Women in Business. She said that a couple of years ago, Julia and Claire were running against one another for president of the regional chapter. Julia pulled out suddenly, so unchallenged, Claire got the appointment."

"So? What's the big deal? Is becoming the president of the association that important?"

"You'll have to ask Julia. I also called my contractor to ask about Claire."

"Is he in the builders association with Amayo?"

"Yes. He usually recommends the Garden Settlement Nursery for landscaping to his home buyers. The nursery had a problem with Claire, and since I know Gene Settle, the owner, I called him." She paused for effect.

"So tell me already. It's getting hot out here."

"Why aren't you inside in the air conditioning?"

"I'm going there as soon as we hang up."

"Then I'll make this fast. Gene said that one of his greenhouses was broken into. Plants were uprooted. Pots smashed to pieces. The sprinkler system was reset to run all night. He lost thousands of dollars in plants and pottery."

"And he thought Claire did it?"

"It was the day after they'd had an argument. She had promised one of her clients that Gene would come by to bid on a landscaping job the next day. He was swamped and told her she should have given the client his number because there was no way he could squeeze in time until later in the week, but if Claire would give him the client's number, he would call and set up an appointment. She said if he wouldn't do it the day her client was expecting him then *ef* him, and stormed out. The next day, Gene walked into his business to find the greenhouse destroyed."

"Crime-o-nee! Did he press charges?"

"He talked to the cops about it, but it didn't go very far. No proof."

"No security cameras?"

"I guess not."

"Too bad."

"Yeah. What do you think?"

"I think Claire made a lot of enemies. I wonder if she had any friends?"

"I can't think of any," Ariana said flatly.

"I'm going to talk to Gary's parents tomorrow if I get a chance. Can you go with me?"

"Too busy. But that reminds me. Guess who called me today?"

"Who?"

"Dawson's mother."

"What did *she* want?"

"To tell me that she'd been mistaken when she spoke with me yesterday. She said that *biao mei* does not mean girlfriend. It means cousin."

"And what about that other phrase that she translated?"

"*Wo ai ni.* That one she got right. It does mean *I love you.*"

"Well, you know, that would make sense," I prodded. "I mean, leaving a message for a cousin that ended 'I love you.'"

"Then why didn't Dawson tell me about his cousin?"

"It probably slipped his mind. Didn't you talk to him?"

"I haven't had time," she said haughtily. "Besides, he's the one that started it. It's up to him."

"You are so pig-headed."

"I know. And proud of it." She was quiet a moment, then said, "Listen, I'm sorry I wasn't there for you yesterday. When you're ready to talk ... well, you know."

"I know." I swallowed a lump in my throat. "Right now, I just want to get Isaac out of jail. He didn't kill Claire." Perspiration was trickling between my boobs. "Damn it's hot out here."

"Go," she said. "I'll talk to you later."

~~~

Val held back the tears until we were in the car. "I had to talk to him through the glass. He couldn't even hold Cody. It's so unfair. *He didn't do it,*" she sobbed. "What if he never gets out?"

I didn't need the waterworks. I'd spent the time in the waiting room dwelling on being attacked by Tony Gardner, worrying about Isaac's incarceration, and fuming about Thurman's Neanderthal attitude. The cry I had built up would wash away a week's worth of dirt from an oil field truck working the King Ranch.

However, several things kept my tears in check. The police were on the lookout for Gardner, and hopefully, he would soon be off the streets; Thurman moved up a rung on the evolutionary ladder—he might be giving me the silent treatment, but it beat the heck out of harassing phone calls; and if I didn't get Valerie settled down, Cody might start crying. He was already starting to make those pouty mouth motions.
~~~

"We're going to get him out," I said.

"How?" She blinked back the tears and looked at me. "We can't pay the bail, and we can't ask you to."

"That's good, because I don't have that kind of money. I didn't mean we were going to get him out this minute, but I know he didn't do it."

"You do?"

"Of course, I do. We just have to prove it to the police."

"Can you do that?"

"Not just yet, but Mrs. Henry, Mrs. Wu, and I are going to find the proof."

"They're going to help Isaac, too?"

"They're already helping."

Her blissful smile of innocence bounced back and filled me with hope until she said, "Can you take me by my house? Isaac reminded me we have some bills I need to pay."

Hope was replaced with terror. I wasn't going near that house. "I need some things at Wal-Mart. Let's go shopping first," I said, playing for time.

It worked. While we were in the store, Thurman called to say he was going to grab dinner at Ray's, so I was able to put the trip to Valerie's house off by telling her we had to meet Thurman. He hadn't actually asked me to meet him. It sounded more like a hostile courtesy call. "Don't worry about cooking supper for me. I'm eating at Ray's." But hostile or not, it was a good excuse to avoid Pleasant Valley and a place even more frightening—my kitchen.

Chapter Twenty-six

Ray's is Ray's Pigskin Barbeque. He also owns Tea and Sympathy and Michelangelo's. Ray's is, of course, a barbecue joint. It takes up most of a large barn-like structure located at the intersection of DeLeon and Navarro, two major thoroughfares. Tea and Sympathy, he opened for his wife. A tearoom and arts and crafts shop combined, Tea and Sympathy caters to the blue-haired ladies lunch crowd and those looking for the unique gift until five o'clock when Debbie closes shop.

Since it was after five and the other end of the parking lot was filling up, I parked in front of the Tea and Sympathy end of the building.

"That's so pretty," Valerie remarked pointing to the ivy stenciling around the front door and display window.

"We'll come back and have lunch one day," I promised. "You'll like the stuff Debbie sells."

"I can't afford to buy anything."

"We'll just look," I said as I led the way into Ray's.

While Debbie's little store is decorated for the more genteel disposition, Ray's Pigskin is football, football, football. Six televisions hang from the open rafters playing football games, replays, or trivia games from opening until closing. Signed jerseys, autographed photos, and trophies cover the walls and display cases. Ray serves his critically acclaimed barbeque on Styrofoam plates. He serves every beer imaginable ice cold—in the bottle, in the can, or on draft.

A dazed Valerie stood at the entrance to the large open dining area taking in the spectacle. I searched the dining area for Thurman, saw him sitting with a few other regulars, and headed toward his table.

He saw me before I reached him and pushed back from the table. "Gotta go, fellas," he said, standing. The sandwich and fries on his plate looked half finished.

I said hello to the men who were with him and told Thurman to finish his dinner, Valerie and I would get another table. He said he had work to do at home.

His chilly reception rubbed me the wrong way. "You don't have to run off on my account," I said, not caring if the others noticed. "Do you think you can avoid me indefinitely?"

"That's not possible is it?" he said, pushing his chair under the table noisily. He threw some money on the table and left.

Valerie looked at me uncomfortably. I glared down at the men who hurriedly returned to their meals.

When we were seated, Valerie asked, "Are you and Mr. Matheson fighting about me? Because I can move back home."

The way she said it nearly broke my heart. "No, sweetheart, we're not fighting about you. And you're not moving home." I couldn't make myself go back to her house, and I sure couldn't let *her* go as long as that scorpion Gardner was around. For Valerie's sake, I needed to clear the air with Thurman as soon as I got home. But *damn,* it was going to be hard.

I held Cody while Valerie went to get a highchair. It's hard to stay mad when you're bouncing a baby on your lap, so by the time Valerie returned, I was feeling better. Val placed the highchair between us. While she wrestled the baby into it, I pulled a toy I'd just purchased from my purse to keep him entertained until the food arrived.

A menu appeared in front of me. "What did you do to the poor man now?" my sister-in-law said teasingly.

I looked up. "I didn't do anything to him. It must be food poisoning," I said with a vicious smile. "What are you doing here? Isn't it quitting time?"

"One of the waitresses didn't show up. I'm filling in."

Turning to Valerie, I said, "This is Debbie Matheson, my sister-in-law. Debbie's the reason I'll never have grandchildren."

Valerie's brow furrowed.

"Hello, darlin'," Debbie said, smiling at Val and patting Cody on the cheek. "Don't pay any attention to her."

"Debbie's influence is what led Marissa to try out for the nunnery," I said.

She looked at me scornfully. "You don't 'try out' like you're going out for the cheerleading squad."

"It's still your fault I don't have grandchildren. If you hadn't persuaded Marissa into joining a cult, she'd be married by now."

Debbie crossed herself. "The Catholic Church is not a cult."

"Then why did it brainwash her into being celibate?"

"She is not brainwashed. She is a nun." Debbie's voice rose in decibels and pitch.

"Exactly. And she would never have become a nun if you hadn't dragged her to mass every time the door was open."

"I didn't have to drag her. She wanted to go. You could have taken her to church if you weren't an *atheist.*"

"I'm not an atheist. I believe in God. And I did take her to church. Before you got a hold of her, I took her to a plethora of churches, so she would have exposure to a wide-range of religions."

"And she chose Catholicism," Debbie said self-righteously.

"Which wouldn't have been bad if she had also not chosen to become a nun. That was your fault," I pointed out. "You took her on a field trip to the convent."

Debbie rolled her eyes then explained to Valerie. "It wasn't a field trip. I went to the convent to buy bread from the sisters. Marissa and my girls went with me." She returned her glare to me. "You should be proud that Marissa decided to become a nun. Besides, you'll be a grandmother one day. There's still Samuel."

"Sam won't stop flying jets long enough to get married."

"Sam probably has children scattered from here to the Mediterranean."

I gasped, "Debbie! I'm shocked. Not that you'd think Sam capable of such a thing, but that you would even have a thought like premarital sex in your head."

"I don't have time for this. The restaurant is filling up, and we're short-handed at the moment."

"I can help," Valerie said meekly. "I'm taking food service at school."

Debbie's expression softened as she turned to Valerie. "That's sweet of you, darlin'," she said. "But it looks like you have your hands full with this little cutie." She patted the baby's cheek.

"His name is Cody."

"Hello, Cody. You're a sweet little boy."

"Oh, sure, go ahead," I said. "Show off your grandmothering skills. You've got grandkids. Your daughters didn't have to take a vow of celibacy."

Debbie glared at me then cast a sunshine smile on Valerie. "You just enjoy having dinner, even if you can't enjoy the company. But if you want a part-time job, come back and see me later on, just don't use *her* as a reference."

"Thanks," Valerie glanced at me, unsure if she should show her pleasure at the job offer.

Debbie scowled at me once more then departed.

Valerie asked, "You don't like the other Mrs. Matheson, do you?"

"I love Debbie. I just like setting her off. It's fun to watch her ears turn red."

"Then you don't really mind Marissa being a nun?"

"Of course not. I want my children to be happy. And Marissa is happy. But don't tell Debbie what I just told you." I winked. "It'll ruin my fun."

We had ordered and were enjoying the first bites of dinner when Tarzan appeared at the table, pulled out a chair, and sat down. "Hey, little guy," he said, gently chucking Cody under the chin before looking at Val and me. "Hello, ladies. You don't mind if I join you, do you?"

"Hi, Mr. Tarzan," Valerie said.

"Just call me Tarzan," he said.

Cody reached his arms out, and Tarzan pulled him onto his lap. Cody grabbed at his beard.

"Did your parents name you that?" Valerie asked.

"Sure did, little lady. I came out swingin' from the rafters."

I rolled my eyes.

"It's true," he said. "Say. What's this I hear about Isaac being tossed in the hoosegow for Claire's murder?"

"He didn't do it," Valerie said defensively.

"I didn't say he did."

"He's in jail because he got mad at the cop."

"I've been mad at a few myself. Was he in a bar fight?"

"Tarzan," I said. "Isaac is under twenty-one."

"That never stopped me."

"We were at home." Valerie told Tarzan what had led up to Isaac's arrest.

I explained why the police had changed the charge to murder then asked, "Do you know anything about Claire Nathe?"

"She had some kind of girlie business. Pillows and that kind of stuff," he explained. "I know Gary from way back. He use to photograph wildlife before he got married. He was good. One of the local galleries carried his stuff when he was still in high school. I guess he had to give it up when the kid's started coming."

"What was Gary like before he got married?"

"Quiet. In the woods a lot. He took pictures for the school newspaper."

"How did he meet Claire?"

"I don't rightly know. He just turned up married." He frowned. "You won't find me in that condition again."

"You say that like marriage is a fatal disease."

"It is for me." He stuck his tongue out of the side of his mouth and rolled his eyes up into his head.

Valerie and Cody laughed.

Tarzan shook off "death" and said, "By the way, I think this is yours." He reached into his shirt pocket and handed me a roll of film.

"Thanks," I said. "How did you end up with it?"

"Susie gave it to me—the girl that borrowed your camera the other night. She put in a new roll of film but forgot to give you the used one when she returned your camera."

I was surprised she'd known how to open it. "I'm glad to have it back. Thanks." I slipped it into my purse hoping it contained another clue.

Chapter Twenty-seven

I was *not* going to Pleasant Valley. I managed to convince Valerie I needed to get home to mow the yard before dark, and I'd take her by her house the next day. The next day, I'd try to come up with another excuse.

Thurman was in his workshop when we got home. We needed to talk, but I didn't bother to interrupt him. I didn't think it was a great idea to try to clear the air when I was still smoldering. For once, I was glad the grass was high.

I suggested to Valerie that she take Cody and Sawdust for a walk, warned her she might see another side of the Sherman boys without Thurman around, and told her to say hi to Mrs. Lyttle for me if she saw her outside. Then I changed into grubbies, filled the riding lawn mower with gas, and started 'er up.

Going round and round and round the yard is hypnotic and rather relaxing, even when the roar of an engine is damaging one's eardrums. I'd made about four circuits around the front yard when the photo of the tuxedo-clad Nathan popped into my head. How often does an eighteen-year-old kid have a reason to wear a tuxedo? To the prom. A wedding? Did he attend so many formal events he had reason to purchase one? I didn't think so. So if he didn't own a tux, how did he get one at such short notice? Or was it short notice? Had he planned on being at the gala? Dressed in a tuxedo in a sea of tuxedos, he wouldn't be noticed. Just one more penguin in the flock. He could have waited until Claire was alone, persuaded her to meet him in the arena, then strangled her. It sounded plausible. Then why was I more sure of Isaac's innocence than Nathan's guilt?

~~~

It was dark when I finally put away the mower and edger. Val had returned from her walk, bathed Cody and put him to bed, taken a shower, and was in her room reading a book. The lights were on in the workshop. Should I go talk to Thurman? I thought about apologizing. Apologize for what? Being in the wrong place at the wrong time? I already did that. For not telling him that it had happened? I'd already apologized for that. *Why should I beg his forgiveness? I didn't attack anyone.*

That went well. I decided to get a shower and put on my nightgown. If anyone was going to apologize around here, it was going to be Thurman.

But he didn't. We spent the night in the same bed a hundred miles apart across a frozen wasteland.

~~~

The morning started out being just as chilly. Thurman sat in his chair at the breakfast table, silently shoveling cereal into his mouth. Valerie quietly coaxed Cody to eat. Luis sat in his usual chair, though he'd been conspicuously absent the day before. I hid behind the newspaper, unable to eat. It was a wonder we all weren't frostbitten.

Valerie broke the ice. "Mrs. Matheson, will we have time to run by my house on the way to school?"

Thurman's spoon clattered into his bowl. The cats, who'd been lying under the table, scrammed. I put down the newspaper. Valerie and Cody stared, wide-eyed, at Thurman.

"After what happened the other night, she's not going back to your house," he said.

"What happened?" Valerie asked.

He looked at me, sharply. "You didn't tell her?"

I shook my head.

"Why not?"

I shrugged.

Valerie hadn't broken the ice. She'd blown up an iceberg.

"If she's old enough to have a baby, she's old enough to hear the word *rape.*"

"I wasn't raped."

"You could have been."

"I wasn't."

"If Valerie had been there instead of you, *she* probably would have been. Doesn't she have the right to know what Tony Gardner did?"

"What did he do?" Valerie asked.

"Until that s.o.b. is arrested, she shouldn't be alone," he said. "He went to that house to rape *her.*"

I started bawling. Valerie started bawling. Cody started bawling. Thurman was still yelling as he wiped away tears. Luis picked up his cereal bowl and walked out of the house.

"You tell Valerie what happened, and you tell her now," Thurman said.

So, through sobs, I told her. I told her everything that had happened, and while I was at it, I told her everything I had been feeling, not only during the attack, but in the days since. All the while I was talking, she interrupted continually to apologize.

I stopped crying and blew my nose. "I shouldn't have

wasted time at the store," I said. "It put me at your house at dark. I knew I shouldn't have gone in."

"I'm sorry," she said for the umpteenth time.

"It's not you're fault," Thurman and I both said at the same time.

I looked into his eyes. There was no more anger. Only hurt. He reached for my hand and held it. "It's not your fault either." That started me bawling again.

Thurman kissed me then handed me his handkerchief.

I finally calmed down. "Valerie, Thurman is right. You shouldn't be at home alone. We don't know whether or not Gardner will come back."

He pushed back from the table and stood up, still holding my hand. "I'll take Valerie to her house, then I'll take her to school. You can pick her up." He pulled my hand to his lips and kissed it. "Valerie, go get your stuff."

So that was that. Thurman had said whatever he needed to say and had heard whatever he needed to hear. I didn't know exactly what it was he'd said and heard, but the Neanderthal had disappeared and my husband had returned.

Valerie picked up Cody and carried him to her room.

"What are you going to do today?" Thurman asked.

I thought about the day I had planned. Buy fertilizer at the garden center, mail the latest Cussler paperback to Samuel, investigate a murder. I looked up at my husband. He finally seemed his calm, in-control self. But I wasn't sure how he would take the news that Ariana, Willi, and I were nosing around in the Nathe murder. I'd hate for him to *de*-evolve.

"Run errands," I said.

~~~

The first "errand" was to KDTX. I arrived a little before nine. As I entered the front door, I was facing a window that looked into the studio where a couple of DJs were working. Their light-hearted banter flowed into the lobby
~~~

from overhead speakers. A receptionist sat at a desk to the right. "May I help you?" she asked.

I told her why I was there and waited while she picked up the phone and dialed a number.

A few moments later a tall, thin red-haired kid bounced into the office. "Hi. You looking for me?"

"If you're Patrick."

"That's me." He reached out his hand and pumped my hand like he was jacking up a car. "I guess you're Mrs. Matheson. You're probably not Raven's mom, because your not black. Not that you couldn't be Raven's mom, but the odds are you're the other lady Raven said was coming to talk to me."

I laughed. Patrick was definitely in the right line of work—*he could talk.* "I see why you're a DJ. And you're right. Mrs. Henry couldn't make it. Do you mind if I ask you a few questions?"

"Not at all." He crossed his arms. "Shoot."

"Can we go somewhere a little more private?"

"Oh, yeah, sure." He bounced down the hall, stopping at a door marked *Conference*, opened the door, and ushered me in.

I sat on one side of the table. He sat on the other and leaned forward with his arms resting on the table. "Raven said you wanted to know about Kamie," he said. "I haven't seen her for years, so I can't tell you how to get in touch with her."

"I know how to reach her. If you're interested, she's home for her mother's funeral."

He held up his left hand and flashed his wedding band. "My wife wouldn't understand."

"Then you won't mind if I ask why you broke up."

He sat up. "Why?"

"I'm trying to understand why someone killed her mother. The boy that was arrested didn't do it. I want to find out who did. Can you shed any light on the situation?"

"I don't know anything about the murder."

"I didn't think you did. But you can tell me a little about the Nathes. Kamie's grandmother said that Kamie ran away from home. Do you know why?"

"Yeah." I felt the table shaking and realized Patrick's leg was bouncing up and down. "But I don't know if I should tell you."

"Did you know that Kamie left here and went to Pasadena?"

"No, I didn't. I figured she would have run farther than that."

"She got a job and went to college. But her mother didn't know that. Her mother thought she had gone to her grandparents. Claire called the grandparents every day harassing them about Kamie. She didn't believe they didn't know where Kamie was. She practically declared war on them, subjecting them to harassing phone calls and abusive letters." The staccato beat his foot played on the floor picked up a pace.

"You're not surprised, are you? Is that why Kamie left? Because of her mother's abuse?"

He rubbed his face with both hands. "Yeah. When Kamie and I were going together, she'd complain about her mom. But I thought it was the normal stuff. I complained about my folks, too. But that's not the way it was. The night she left, Kamie came to my house. She wanted me to run away with her. I told her I couldn't. I was already working here at the station; it was in the wee hours of the morning when no one was listening, but at least I was on the air. Kamie told me her mom had taken her keys and she was stuck unless I'd go with her. I told her her mom would give in sooner or later, and she could have her car back."

"She ran away because her mom took away the car?"

"She ran away because her mom killed her cat."

"What?"

"When Kamie told me, I thought her mom had run over it by accident. But that wasn't it. Kamie's mom had been checking the mileage on her car. She told her she knew she was lying about where she'd been. She and Kamie had a big fight and Kamie told her that she'd been to see her grandparents, that she'd been going to visit them a lot, and she was going to continue visiting them. Kamie was pretty hard-headed.

Her mom hit the ceiling. She said she'd teach Kamie about disobeying. She went into Kamie's room, picked up her cat and slammed it against the wall."

I felt nauseous. It wasn't *bug guts* nauseous. It was overwhelming disgust. "Why didn't you tell someone?"

"I felt guilty for not taking Kamie away when she wanted me to, and Kamie asked me not to. She said if I wasn't going to help her, the least I could do was keep my mouth shut and not ruin her good reputation." He laughed. "She meant her tough reputation." He grew quiet a moment, then said, "Kamie stood up to anyone who ever crossed her. I thought she could take care of herself. It turns out she could. Do you think Kamie did it?"

"I haven't had a chance to talk to Kamie directly, and I don't want to jump to conclusions. Did Claire contact you after Kamie disappeared?"

"She came over the next day. I told her I didn't know where Kamie went, but I knew why, and if she bothered me again, I'd tell Dad."

"Your dad is Judge Harold Koontz?"

"Yeah."

"I guess you didn't have any more trouble with Claire."

"Nope."

But Mildred and Bernie did.

Chapter Twenty-eight

If Claire called her own mother when Kamie ran away, it would make sense she would call Gary's parents. I asked the receptionist at KDTX if I could borrow her phone book and looked up the address.

The Gary Nathe, Srs., lived on a heavily traveled street in an older section of Dulcinea. The front yard had been eaten away to practically nothing when Mesquite Avenue was expanded to four lanes. I pulled the Suburban into the driveway and hoped a passing car wouldn't take off my bumper.

I was acting on Willemina's advise: pop in like Columbo. I wasn't comfortable popping in. No more comfortable than I had been through any of this mess. In the last few days, I'd pried into more private areas than a gynecologist.

I rang the bell anyway. The door was opened by a woman who was probably in her mid-sixties. From the family resemblance, I could be ninety-nine percent sure she was Gary's mother.

I introduced myself. "I worked with Claire on the benefit for the Performing Arts Center. I hope you don't mind that I dropped by to tell you how sorry I am about her death." I also hoped she wouldn't guess correctly that I'd had to do a little research in order to know where to drop by.

"Then you've met Ariana!" she exclaimed.

The rich and famous connection was finally going to pay off. "I've known Ariana for years. We're best friends." Maybe this was going to be easy after all.

She threw her arms open wide and hugged me like I was *her* best friend. "Darling, come in. Claire told me she worked side-by-side with Ariana on several occasions. She said Ariana respected her decorating suggestions and had even recommended her to her New York connections."

That was news to me, and I bet it would have been news to Ariana. I was glad she wasn't along. She would have demolished that lie like a *piñata* at a ten-year-old's birthday party.

I stepped into the living room. It was furnished in Queen Anne. A curiosity cabinet held a collection of Lladro figurines. Other Lladro, along with framed photos, sat on crocheted doilies covering the coffee table. The photos were autographed pictures—Linda Evans, Kenny Rogers, Michael Douglas. More autographed photos covered the walls. "Ariana is very generous to the people and causes she believes in," I said. That wasn't a lie. She was generous, but Claire wasn't one of the causes Ariana believed in.

"I know." She put her hand to her chest. "I mean, I don't know her *personally,* but she has *an air* of benevolence about her." With a flourish, she motioned to the nearest chair. "Please sit down."

Mrs. Nathe wore a peach long-sleeved jacket with black piping, a peach and black striped shell and black skirt, pearl necklace and over-sized earrings, hose, and black pumps.

I had dressed for the heat. I wore a yellow, light-weight

pants set with comfortable sandals. "Am I keeping you from something?" I asked.

"I was going shopping, but I can go later. You know, I would just love to meet Ariana."

"I'd be happy to introduce you," I said. Shopping? I didn't dress that well when I was teaching. I certainly didn't dress up to go shopping. I felt like I was sitting in front of Joan Collins.

"You know, my granddaughter works with someone famous."

"Really?"

I thought I heard a snort in the next room.

She apparently didn't hear it. She leaned forward and put her well-manicured hand up in a stop-and-listen-to-this gesture. "She works for a director in Hollywood. He's some kind of foreigner. I never can remember how to pronounce his name. He did that picture about the little boy who saw dead people." She gave a little shiver for effect.

"M. Night Shyamalan?" I'd seen the director promoting one of his flicks on television. His accent wasn't foreign. It sounded Californian to me. But maybe Mrs. Nathe thought Californians were foreign.

"That's it. I don't care for that kind of movie, but I think it's just wonderful that she has such an exciting career."

"That is exciting," I said. Heck, even I was impressed. "How many grandchildren do you have?" I asked.

"Two. Gary's two children. He's an only child."

"Kamie works for M. Night Shyamalan? I thought she lived in Pasadena?"

"California?"

"Texas."

"Pasadena, Texas? I should say not. She lives in Malibu, darling."

There was that snort again. Either I was hearing things, or Mrs. Nathe chose to ignore it.

"Claire said Kamie's going to get us passes, so we can actually watch while they're filming the next movie."

Kamie was running a hotel in Texas one day and making movies in California the next. So who was living in la-la land, Mildred or *Joan?* I was betting on *Joan.* The least I could do was call her by her real name. From all the autographed photos that read *To Victoria—*, I made an educated guess. "Mrs. Nathe, do you mind if I call you Victoria?"

"Not at all." She jumped up. "I've forgotten my manners. Let me get you something to drink." She hurried into the kitchen. I heard ice clinking against glass and soon she was back. She handed me a tumbler of iced tea then returned to her seat. "Tell me about Ariana. What was it like working in New York?"

Victoria seemed to accept me as Ariana's proxy, so I recalled some of the things she'd told me about living in New York. I left out the first year Ariana modeled when culture shock nearly brought her home. I thought about the losers she had dated, lived with, and married. I decided Mrs. Nathe would be more interested in the exotic locales Ariana visited.

I didn't tell her there was seldom time for sightseeing. Ariana would be flown in and flown out of a city, sometimes on the same day. I remember how disappointed she was her second year with the agency when she thought she was going to spend time in Rome. She called me and ticked off everything she wanted to see: the Colosseum, St. Peter's, the Pantheon, the catacombs.... But she was kept so busy, she had time only to check out her immediate surroundings. She came home disappointed and exhausted. Ariana eventually made it back to Rome on her own. She took the time to see everything she'd missed on her first trip, and she took the time to recover from her breakup with Kevin the Casanova.

I decided Victoria would enjoy hearing about Rome, with some embellishment. I put Ariana in fabulous outfits, stationed her in each of the locales she eventually visited, and draped her on the arms of hollywood hunks of Mrs. Nathe's generation—Robert Wagner, Paul Newman, Sean Connery. She sat on the edge of her seat as if she were a spectator at a sporting event.

"When Ariana returned from Rome, she toured New England on a layout for *Glamour Magazine* on the Ivy League schools," I said. "You know, Princeton, Harvard, Columbia, Yale...."

She sat up and smoothed her skirt. "My grandson, Nathan, is going to Harvard this year. He's going to law school. I expect after he passes his bar exam, he'll be asked to join a very prestigious firm. He's very bright."

"Why did he choose law over math?" I asked. "I understand he's truly gifted in mathematics."

"Math? What can he become with a math degree? A teacher? What's so great about that?"

I took a deep breath and was about to let her know in no uncertain terms what was great about being a teacher, when I heard another snort coming from the other room and the rustle of a newspaper being fanned and folded. A man, whom I took to be Gary's dad, shuffled into sight. He wore an undershirt, wrinkled khaki shorts, and bedroom slippers. He looked our way, grunted, shook his head and shuffled down the hall.

Mrs. Nathe watched him until she heard a door close. "Don't mind him. As I was saying, Nathan is going to be a lawyer. We have Claire to thank for that. She finally convinced him he would have a much better future if he put that silly math thing aside."

"You and Claire were close?"

"Oh, yes. She was the best thing that ever happened to us. It was through her L.A. connections that I received all of these photographs. That's how Claire got Kamie a job in Hollywood—through a friend of a friend. Gary has Claire to thank for his life as a celebrated portrait photographer."

Gary was good, but celebrated? "I heard that he also photographed wildlife." I said.

She tsk-tsked. "That was just a phase he went through when he was young. How was he going to make a living taking pictures of deer? Claire got him on the right track. She was good for him. She knew how important it was to maintain one's stature in the community."

Chapter Twenty-nine

Stature was very important to Claire. It probably motivated her to run for president of Women in Business.

When I left the Nathe's house, I called Julia Thompson at work. I was so into the Ariana's proxy role, I almost used it on her. But I didn't. If Julia dropped out of the race because of Claire, she'd already been jerked around by a big fake. I figured the truth would be a much better ploy.

I introduced myself. "A friend of mine suggested I speak with you. She said you were in Women in Business with Claire Nathe."

There was a drawn out silence on the other end of the phone, and I was beginning to think I should have gone with the "famous friend" tactic.

"If you're looking for someone to eulogize Claire Nathe, you'll have to look to someone else. I won't be shedding any tears."

"Wait," I said, afraid she was going to hang up. "I heard you ran against her for president. I was given the impression that she did something to cause you to drop your name from the list of candidates."

"It's not something I want to discuss."

"Ms. Thompson, the boy that is being held for Claire Nathe's murder is innocent. I'm trying to find out everything I can about Claire in order to free him. Please talk to me."

She considered it a moment. "I haven't eaten yet. Meet me at Red Lobster at twelve-thirty. You can buy my lunch. I'm wearing red."

~~~

I had time to drop off the roll of film at the drive-through photo joint and ship Sam's book at UPS. I arrived at the restaurant before Julia and waited on a bench for about five minutes when a woman in a red dress walked in. She was tall and slim with blonde hair and probably in her mid-thirties.

We were seated at a booth where a black and white photo of a shrimp trawler hung on the wall over the condiments and dessert menu. I was considering the Fudge Overboard as my main entree when the waiter arrived to take our drink order. Julia ordered chardonnay. I ordered the same.

"Why are you interested in Claire Nathe?" she asked. I explained about Isaac's arrest and my connection to him. She listened quietly then suggested we look over the menu.

When she closed hers, I told her what Claire had done to an employee of Gary's. "I don't want to name names," I said. "The employee swears if it was drugs, it wasn't hers. That Claire planted the drugs to force her to quit her job."

The waiter returned with our drinks. Julia took a long sip of her wine, then we ordered our food. I settled on flounder, a pathetic substitute for brownies and ice cream.

When the waiter left, I said, "Claire may have had something to do with destroying the property of a business owner
~~~

she was angry with. Was she angry with you for running against her?"

"I think she would have been angry at anyone who ran against her. Anyone with a chance of winning."

"Becoming the president of an organization is a lot of work. Why did you run?"

"The position of president puts you in contact with a lot of people: people in finance, in the media, people who can help your business grow."

"Then why drop out of the race?"

She twirled the wine glass by its stem. "I had to weigh the benefit of contacts I could make by becoming president of the organization against the damage any accusation could do to my business and family."

"What kind of accusation?"

"A false one. Claire said if I ran against her, she would expose a family secret. We have no family secrets, but she said she'd invent one."

"If it was conjured out of thin air, why not just deny it?"

"That was my first inclination. But she reminded me about J.D. Woodard. She had a portrait studio here about ten years ago."

"Yes. I remember," I said. "I was surprised when it closed."

"A rumor started that J.D. was having an affair with her female assistant. She denied the affair. Her assistant denied the affair. They denied being lesbians. But the damage had already been done. Her marriage was destroyed. Her business was destroyed. J.D. left town. The assistant found another job here in town, but the shadow still follows her, even though she's married now."

"That's awful."

"The real shame is this—it was bogus. Claire started the rumor."

"How do you know?"

"She told me, indirectly. She said, 'Poor J.D. Woodard. Isn't it interesting how asking a few carefully selected questions can plant an idea that will spread through town like wildfire? People will believe anything. They love a scandal. Poor J.D. I guess we'll never really know.'"

She crossed her arms and leaned toward me. "I knew J.D. I'd never imagined she was anyone other than what I saw, a woman trying to run her business and take care of her family just like me, so I was floored when I heard the rumor, but even I began to believe it after I'd heard it over and over again. And then when her husband filed for divorce.... Well, that just finished it off. There was no way she was going to recover in this town."

I thought of the high-profile sports figure who'd been accused of rape a few years back. He was tried in the media long before the case went to court, as was his accuser.

"I'm not stupid, Darby. I didn't want to end up like J.D. I dropped out of the race and out of the organization." Julia swallowed the last of her wine. "Like I said, I won't be shedding any tears."

~~~

After lunch, I thanked Julia for taking time to talk to me, then headed back to the photo shop to pick up the pictures. I pulled into a parking space and searched through each one hoping to discover something that would lead me to Claire's killer. I found nothing.

I called Ariana's number. She didn't answer, but I left a message relaying what Julia had told me.

Then I called Willi.

"I have found no connection between Claire Nathe and Dean Moss or Sherilyn Rather," she said.

"Who?"

"The people you asked about at lunch yesterday. The ones in the picture with Gary. There's no connection. But I was thinking, what about Gary?"
~~~

"Gary? I didn't even consider Gary." Well, maybe I did, but it was just a fleeting thought. "He's so ... *nice.*"

"I know. It's hard for me to think he killed her, either. But when the police are looking at suspects they look at the spouse first."

"How do you know?"

"Look at Marlena. She was nice. But hiding behind that sweet façade was a murderer itching to get out. She tried to kill Alice. Of course, it wasn't her fault."

"Ga-a-ag," I said. "You earned a masters in art history at one of the finest universities in this country, and you still waste your time watching that crap."

"And the mystery series you buy in bulk aren't crap?"

"They are art and entertainment," I said.

"As are my soaps. About Gary. He had the opportunity. He could have slipped away any time."

"So find out if he did. His prop could tell you—the boy dressed as the Queen's Guard."

"I've been trying to reach him. So far I've been unsuccessful, but I'll let you know when I do."

"Great," I said. "And, Willi, maybe your soap operas aren't crap."

"Of course not. You watch them."

"I do not!"

"Then how did you know Marlena and Alice were soap opera characters?"

~~~

I had a hankering for chocolate, so I drove through the Dairy Queen and ordered an M&M Blizzard. I parked under a tree, left the motor running, and added a few inches to my waistline.

The phone rang about the time I needed to come up for air. I put my dessert in the cup holder and reached for the phone. It was Valerie calling from school.

"Thank you, Mrs. Matheson. Thank you. Thank you
~~~

for getting Isaac out of jail. He'll be here in a few minutes to pick me up."

"Wait a minute, Valerie. I didn't get Isaac out."

"You didn't?"

"I told you. I don't have that kind of money."

"That's okay. Somebody paid his bond. I don't care who did. At least he's getting out of jail."

I could think of only two people who could come up with twenty-five thousand dollars. It was unlikely that Willemina would post bond and just as unlikely that Ariana would, though of the two of them, Ariana has a hell of a lot more money but absolutely no reason to bail Isaac out. But something was telling me she did.

"He's picking me up in just a few minutes."

"Where are you going?"

"Home. He's ready to go home. You've been great, but I'm ready to go home, too."

I panicked. What about Gardner? What if Gardner comes back? What if Valerie tells Isaac that Gardner made advances toward her and he decides to pull a Thurman and go after him? "Come out to my house," I pleaded. "You have to pick up your stuff anyway. What about Cody's nebulizer? He'll need his breathing treatments."

"I brought it to school with me. He has to have treatments at noon. I can pick everything else up later. Isaac's here. Thanks, again. I'll call you tomorrow."

Chapter Thirty

I called Thurman and told him Isaac was released on bond, that he was picking Valerie up at school, and they were going to their house. "What if Valerie tells him about Tony Gardner attacking me? What if she tells Isaac he had been coming on to her? Isaac might do something stupid and get himself thrown back in jail."

"Calm down," he said. "Where are you?"

"At the Dairy Queen on Bridge Street."

"Stay there. I'll meet you. Order me a chocolate shake."

~~~

I cooled my heels for the fifteen minutes or so it took for him to arrive then rode with him in his truck to Pleasant Valley. When we pulled in front of their house, I forced myself to get out of the truck. Thurman took my hand and helped me up the broken steps onto the porch and up to the door.

"You okay?" he asked.

I nodded.
~~~

He put his arm around my waist. "I'm right here."

Isaac opened the door. Cody stood beside him with one hand holding his daddy's leg. Valerie smiled at us from the middle of the living room.

Isaac shook Thurman's hand. "Thank you, Mr. Matheson and thank you, Miss." He hugged me. "I hated being in there. I'm going to pay you back, I promise." He stepped back. "Come in."

"We didn't bail you out," Thurman said. Then he looked at me. "We didn't, *did we?*"

"No. I swear. I told Valerie it wasn't us."

Isaac offered us a seat on the lowrider couch then went into the kitchen and returned with a dinette chair for himself and Valerie.

"Whoever got me out, I'm sure glad. I called Carlos, and he said he didn't do it, but he sure needs me back at work, so I'm going tomorrow. I'm glad I still have a job. I was afraid he was going to fire me."

"You're innocent until proven guilty, Isaac," I said.

"The cops don't think so. But all they had to do was ask Carlos. I was busy the whole night."

"The police probably think Carlos couldn't watch you the entire time. They put together the evidence they needed. You threatened Mrs. Nathe. You were at the benefit. Your fingerprints were on the belt."

"I helped Mrs. Wu put stuff in the dressing rooms. I probably touched it then."

Cody toddled over to Thurman, climbed up into his lap, and handed him a book.

"Several people touched it, me included, but the argument you had with Claire and your shoving match with the police clinched it for them."

"I didn't do it."

"We know," Thurman said. "We need to discuss something else." He told Isaac about Tony Gardner while Val and I listened quietly. "Gardner didn't know my wife was going to be here. He thought Valerie would be alone."

Isaac flew off the chair, his fists clenched. "That son-of-a-bitch! I'll kill him."

Thurman stood up slowly and put a hand on Isaac's shoulder. "I know how you feel. Come on, son, let's go outside."

He led Isaac to the door. They jumped off the porch and walked over to the truck.

Val and I peeked out. Thurman leaned against the truck and spoke too low for us to hear. Isaac paced back and forth, punching the air and talking loud enough that we could tell every other word started with an *f*.

Val closed the door.

I spent the time playing with the baby and trying to convince Valerie to bring her family to our house to stay.

Finally, the door opened. "Would you do that, Mr. Matheson?" Isaac asked, leading the way into the living room.

"No, son. I'd probably kick his ass again. But that's not what I want you to do. Someone spent a lot of money getting you out of jail. We want you to stay out. At least, until my nosy wife and her friends can find out how to keep you out permanently."

Chapter Thirty-one

"I wish the kids had come out to the house," I said. We were on our way back to pick up my Suburban.

"They have a home."

"I know. But I'd feel better if they weren't staying there, at least for a while."

"They'll be okay. I told Isaac to call me if he needed anything."

"You meant if Gardner shows up."

We passed the site where the Performing Arts Center was to be built. "I meant for anything," Thurman said.

"How did you know?" I asked.

"How did I know what you and your meddling *amigas* are up to?"

"Well, I wouldn't put it that way, but yes."

"I've got spies."

"Are your spies named Richard and Dawson?"

He grinned but didn't confirm. "I heard you think Nathan did it."

Now how did he hear that? *Did Nathan call him?* No. *Did Willi?* Willi wouldn't have called him. "Nathan could have done it," I said. "I have a picture proving he was at the—*ah, ha!* The chief called you."

"He's just one spy. I need more than one to keep you out of trouble."

I stuck my tongue out at him.

He laughed. "Save it. You can use it later." He pulled into the Dairy Queen and parked next to the Suburban. I started to open the door, but Thurman put his hand on my shoulder. "I know you feel you have to help Isaac, but I want you to be careful. Don't put yourself in a dangerous situation."

"I won't," I said, opening the door.

"Darby," he said, "I'm serious. Pay attention to your ESP this time."

"I don't have ESP."

"Then pay attention to your common sense."

"I promise I'll pay attention to my common sense."

"Good. Now, follow me home."

"But I need to go—"

"Home," he said.

~~~

Thurman spent the rest of the afternoon and early evening working in his workshop. I worked on the business accounts until it was time to fix supper, and when it was ready, set up TV trays so Thurman could watch a poker tournament on Bravo while we ate. When we were finished, I straightened up the kitchen then went to the utility room to clean out the litterbox.

I was head down and ass up when I heard Thurman yell for me. I straightened and yelled out the door, "What is it?"

"What are you doing?"

"Digging for diamonds. What do you want?"
~~~

"When you get done, come here."

I finished cleaning up after the cats, washed my hands, and went back to the family room.

He turned off the TV and stood up. "Let's go."

"Where?"

"There's a full moon. Let's go for a ride."

~~~

It was a beautiful night. The moon was low in the clear night sky. I sat next to Thurman on the bench seat. He drove with one hand on the wheel and the other resting on my shoulder. We rode away from the city and light pollution until we were about fifteen miles out, then turned off the highway and crossed a cattle gap. Thurman drove a little ways in then pulled off the dirt road and parked next to a stock tank surrounded by mesquite trees.

"Whose property is this?" I asked.

"Old Man Kilgore's."

He turned off the lights, rolled down the windows, and turned off the engine. We were still close enough to the highway to hear cars passing.

"It's kind of hot out here," I said.

"It's going to get hotter."

"Are we going to get shot for trespassing?"

"Kilgore's family moved him into a nursing home. Nobody's out here."

"Then why are we?" It was a rhetorical question.

"We need a change of scenery." The moonlight lit up the inside of the truck and illuminated Thurman's face and his intentions. His hand slithered down my shirt.

Smooth isn't a word I'd use to describe a woodcrafter's fingers. But skillful is. My eyelids closed involuntarily as his fingers did a little purposeful roaming, and my body went as limp as a sugar cookie dipped in milk. He pushed the lever on the steering wheel with his left hand, and it popped up out of the way, giving him room to maneuver.
~~~

He kissed my neck, my ear, my cheek, my eyes, my nose, my lips.

"Where's that tongue you were showing off earlier?" he breathed. He kissed my mouth again, and I let him find it. We sank sideways until I was lying flat on my back on the front seat. Thurman raised up, reached back, and opened the driver's side door. He stepped out, struggled out of his clothes, and crawled back onto the seat. He crouched above me on his hands and knees. "Your turn," he said.

I unbuttoned my shirt, released the front clasp on the bra, and peeled the cups back. Thurman buried his face between my breasts. I was floating away on a cloud of sensuous delight when three heart-stopping clangs shot through the truck.

"What the hell?" Thurman yelled, struggling up.

"Something hit the side of the truck," I said.

A beam from a flashlight played across the dashboard.

"Jesus Christ, somebody's out there." He flew backward off the seat and grabbed for the clothes he'd laid across the side of the bed. "Where the hell are my clothes?" he roared.

The light beam hit Thurman straight on. "Looking for these?" an amused voice said. "You know you're trespassing, sir."

I wrestled my boobs into my bra, but closing the clasp was impossible at this angle. "Who is it?" I hissed.

"Sheriff's deputy, Ma'am."

I wanted to melt into the floorboard.

The deputy stepped up to Thurman, handed him his clothes, and shined the beam on me—lying on the front seat of the truck, with both hands unsuccessfully holding my bra together, looking up between my knees into the flashlight.

"Mrs. Matheson?" the deputy said. "Hey. That is you. It's me. Chuck Dechert."

Crap! This was going from bad to worse. "Oh—uh—

hi, Chuck. Meet my husband Thurman. Honey, Chuck graduated from Chapman a few years back."

Chuck lowered the flashlight and turned to shake hands. I struggled to a sitting position and leaned over to get my bra closed, while Thurman used one hand to hold up his pants and the other to shake hands with Chuck.

"Sorry to ruin your evening folks, but this is private property." He grinned. "You'll have to find another place to park." He tipped his hat. "It was nice to see you again Mrs. Matheson. Mr. Matheson."

~~~

I buckled up on the passenger side and didn't say a word. If I opened my mouth, I'd light into Thurman like a swarm of piss ants. "Nobody's out here," he'd said. Somebody was out there! It was embarrassing as hell getting caught *in the act.* And by a former student!

At least I hadn't been completely naked like Thurman. I considered his viewpoint. Poor man, he was probably ready to die of shame, too. Between the disappointment of an interrupted tryst and unbearable embarrassment, he was probably feeling pretty lousy.

He wasn't.

He chuckled. "You should have seen your face. You turned ten-shades of red." He snorted. "And your expression when the deputy identified himself—complete horror." He laughed so hard I thought he'd choke.

"And what about you?" I said. "Standing out there in your birthday suit."

He laughed even harder.

It *was* funny. Embarrassing—but funny. "It would have made a good *Funniest Home Videos,*" I said, smiling. "I hope we don't end up on television. You know they put cameras in patrol cars."

"Well, if we do, I hope I was showing my best side."

I giggled. "You were showing every side."
~~~

I unsnapped the seatbelt and moved next to him. He put his arm around me and I snuggled close. "Life with you is never boring, Thurman Matheson."

"Nor with you, my sweet wife. Nor with you."

Chapter Thirty-two

When we arrived home, Thurman suggested we pick up where we'd left off. I told him it was too late. The spell was broken, the mood was gone, and I wasn't going to get it back.

He changed my mind.

~~~

The next morning, over breakfast, I asked, "Have you ever cheated on me?"

"No. Why do you ask that?"

"Richard cheated on Willi."

"With who?"

"I don't know. Willi said it was back when they were first married."

"Oh?"

"You don't think it's a big deal?"

"I guess it wasn't. They're still married."

"I think it's a big deal. It changes my view of Richard."

"You've known Richard for nearly thirty years. Don't
~~~

let something he did as a kid change your opinion of him."

"I can't help it."

He took a bite of egg, chased it with orange juice, then asked, "What's your opinion of Jerome Steele?"

"I wish he'd find another line of work."

"Is Isaac in the same line of work?"

"No. He might have been a few years ago. I know he and Jerome were tight. That's why Jerome was looking in on Valerie. But Isaac really likes his job, and I think Carlos drug tests his employees, so he's not using. Isaac's trying to make a better life for himself."

"If Isaac's going to make a better life, he's going to have to cut the ties to Jerome. And I'd feel better if you kept your distance from him."

"Jerome's not an evil person."

"Naw. The kid's got some good in him. But he's picked a life that puts him in the cross hairs. That makes it dangerous for everyone around him. Keep that in mind."

"I've thought about it. A lot. One day at school, Jerome and some other students debated legalization of drugs. Jerome said he was against it because it would put the dealers out of business. He didn't admit to being a dealer, but he did ask 'where else can you make that kind of money?' I told him if he went to college he could graduate at twenty-two and have a great job by the time he was twenty-five. He said he wasn't talking about himself, but he didn't expect to live to be twenty-five anyway. I'm afraid he may be right."

"That's why Isaac needs to distance himself from Jerome. He has a better chance, because he has a different attitude."

"It's too bad they have to live in that dump," I said dismally then perked up. "I've got an idea. We could put a little trailer in the back pasture, and they could move in."

Thurman shook his head. "Uh, uh. I'm not adopting them."

I put on my sad-puppy face.

"No, Darby. No way."

I picked up my coffee cup and leaned back. "Oh, well. I tried." And I wasn't through trying.

He looked at me for a long moment then said, "Tell you what. I'll talk to Isaac and find out what it will take to make that place a little more livable."

I smiled. "You're a saint."

"I'm an ain't?"

"YOU ARE A SSSS-AINT."

"I know."

~~~

After breakfast, Thurman went to the shop to get in a few hours of work before we had to get dressed for Claire's funeral. I carried a cup of coffee, the newspaper, and a telephone to the back porch and settled in a lounge chair with Sawdust to keep me company. Blue and the cattle had wandered to the back pasture. A cranky mockingbird made kamikaze passes at Agatha and Melrose as they climbed on the woodpile stacked next to the barn.

I called Ariana. "Are you going to the funeral? It's at eleven."

"I know. I was planning on it."

"Is Dawson going with you?"

"Who knows?"

"You're still not talking?"

"He's in Waco, presumably with his *cousin*—the one he didn't talk to me about."

"Why haven't you called him, especially after his mother told you that it was his cousin, not girlfriend, that called?"

"Number one." This was not a good sign. When Ariana enumerates, she can't be swayed with a hurricane. "His mother doesn't know who called. She simply said *biao mei* means cousin. Do I believe her? I don't know. Why should I? She hates me. Maybe she knows Dawson is having an
~~~

affair, and she's trying to cover it up. How would I know? Number two. Why didn't Dawson tell me he was renting an apartment? Number three. I still don't know who the apartment is for. Number four—"

"Number four," I said. "If you don't talk to Dawson, you'll never know the answers to one, two, or three."

"*Four*—"

"At least ask him if he's going to attend the funeral. If you show up in one car and he shows up in the other and you sit on opposite sides of the church, you're going to start rumors."

"You have a point. I'll ask him if he plans on attending the funeral, but that's all."

"Good." At least that was a start. "Now," I said, "thank you for bailing Isaac out of jail."

"You're welcome."

"You *did* bail him out. I was just guessing."

"I couldn't very well leave *el pobrecito* sitting in jail, could I?"

"I was saying, just yesterday, how generous you are to the *pobrecitos* of the world."

"It has nothing to do with generosity. I need you to go with me to Vegas to do a little *Feng Shui* for my new store, and I know you won't go as long as you're babysitting. Besides, I talked to Carlos. He can't hold Isaac's job indefinitely, and if Isaac loses his job, you'll end up taking in Valerie and her kid. That will put a damper on *my* style."

"Whatever your reasoning is, others will still see it as generous."

"*Others* aren't going to know. Neither are Isaac and Valerie. I put up the bond anonymously. You know I did it because you're *una síquica*."

"It doesn't take a psychic to figure it out. Just common sense. You're the one around here with the big bucks. By the way, I don't do *Feng Shui*. I can barely pronounce it."

"I still expect you to go with me to Vegas. The realtor has several places for me to check out. I want you to go to see if there are any evil spirits lurking about."

"I'm not a witch doctor, either."

"Just stand in the middle of the damn store and meditate. If something hits you, let me know."

"I'll have to talk to Thurman about it. He might want to go, too. Is that okay?"

"Sure," she said. "Hold on." She was quiet a moment then said, "Dawson's pulling in the drive. I'll see you at the funeral."

"Wait a minute. When do you want to go to Vegas? Because I don't want to take off with this thing hanging over Isaac."

"This *thing* could last a year or two," Ariana said.

"I don't think so."

"Really? Is it your *bug guts* again?"

"Not *bug guts,* more like a giant vise tightening around my insides."

"So what's causing it?"

"The same thing that started it—the Nathes."

Chapter Thirty-three

I walked out to the shop. A large tablet lay on the drafting table where Thurman sat, and he sketched as *My Maria* poured out of the radio.

I looked over his shoulder. A trout and redfish swam in an underwater Eden. "What's that going to be?" I asked.

"A wall panel for a bank in Rockport."

"Yeah? How big?"

"The final piece is going to be fifteen feet long. Five feet high. It's going in behind the tellers. These are preliminary sketches." He flipped through the tablet revealing other sketches he'd done. A blue heron with a perch in it's bill. A crab crawling along the ocean floor. "I'm just getting started," he said. "I might use these. We'll see."

I kissed him. "Do you think you can squeeze in a trip to Las Vegas?"

"Are we going to Vegas?"

I told him about Ariana's plans. "She hasn't set a date, but I expect it will be soon. What do you think?"

"Do we have the money?"

"Depends on how much you're going to win or lose."

"You mean, how much *you* are going to win or lose."

"I'll stick to the nickel slots. When are you shipping the wildebeest and lions?"

He looked over at the unfinished table. "Not for a month or so."

"I think we can still swing it." I grinned. "If I stick to the penny slots."

He went back to his sketch. "Then it's fine with me."

The desk phone rang, and I picked it up. "Hello?"

"Is this Jessica Fletcher?" It was Jim Swanson.

"Cute, Chief. What can I do for you?"

"I've got some good news. Tony Gardner's locked up."

I sat down. "He is? That's an enormous relief. Thank you."

"Who is what?" Thurman asked, putting down his pencil.

"Gardner. He's been arrested."

He nodded toward the phone. "Punch the speaker button."

"Hold on, Chief." I pressed *speaker* and replaced the handset. "Go ahead, we're both listening."

"He was where you said he'd be. We picked him up at his girlfriend's house."

"What took so long?" asked Thurman.

"The first time we checked it out, the girlfriend had some cock-and-bull story about him leaving town on business. We were afraid he skipped out. But the detective, Tracy Williams, told Ms. Ybarra we wanted to question Gardner about the assault done *to* him. That we'd heard he'd been beaten up pretty badly by a jealous husband. Tracy said a woman claimed she was assaulted, but she thought the woman was fooling around with Gardner, got caught by her husband, and was trying to cover it up by telling her old man that Gardner had attacked her. Tracy told Ybarra that Gardner was just an innocent guy who hooked up with the wrong woman."

I was horrified. "That's not what happened!"

"We know. But Ybarra bought it. It didn't take long for her to find him and get him to come back to the house. And when he did, she lit into him. They were going at it pretty good when our guys broke 'em up. We ran his prints through AFIS. He's wanted for a sexual assault in San Antonio and another in China Grove. The China Grove victim was fourteen."

"I should have killed him," Thurman said.

"I know how you feel, friend," the chief said, "but I'm glad you didn't. I don't want to lose a fishing partner. Gardner and his lawyer wanted to press charges against you, but I told them it wouldn't fly in court. We had a witness to the assault, and no jury in this town would take Gardner's word over that of a retired school librarian."

"Am I going to have to testify against him?" I asked.

"Bexar County wants to have a go at him first. Their D.A. might ask you to testify for them. It won't be right away, but don't be surprised if you don't get a call from San Antonio."

"Is there a chance he'll get out on bond?"

"None. But that reminds me: your little buddy Isaac Molina is off the hook."

"We know he's out on bail," Thurman said.

"I'm talking about Nathan Nathe. He turned himself in. He confessed to killing his mother."

Chapter Thirty-four

"You're batting a thousand," Thurman said on the way to the funeral. He wore the same suit he'd worn the night of the benefit. I see no sense in exposing more than one garment to death, so I always wear the same dress to funerals. When my funeral dress soaks up too much sorrow and despair, out it goes.

"You were right," he said. "You were right about where the cops would find Gardner, and you were right about Nathan. Your ESP must be working overtime."

"I don't have ESP," I said. "Gardner's whereabouts were a given. He was living with Val's mom. And Nathan, I don't understand. I never thought he'd confess to killing Claire."

"Why not? You suspected him, didn't you?"

"Not really. I thought it was odd that he showed up at the benefit dressed to the nines just to drop off camera equipment for his dad," I said. "He's so shy, he's nearly invisible. I feel sorry for him."

"It's the quiet ones you've got to watch."

We took Main Street to Commerce, then turned left and found a parking space along the curb about a block from Grace Baptist Church.

Thurman opened the door for me, and I got out and linked my arm in his.

Willemina was standing at the front door of the church. I waved and caught her eye. The couple she had been talking to shook hands with her before entering the church, then Willi descended the stairs and met us on the sidewalk. She wore a navy silk dress with a three-tiered hem and matching three-inch heels.

"Where's Richard?" I asked.

"In surgery. Did you hear? Nathan surrendered to the police. Everyone's talking about it."

"The chief called us this morning. I can't believe it."

"She doesn't think he did it," Thurman said.

"You're not serious?" Willi said. "This is what we hoped for. It proves Isaac is innocent."

"That's the only good thing. I can't see Nathan strangling his mother."

"You never can tell about someone." She glanced toward the church. "We'd better get inside. I hear the music starting. Do you mind if I sit with you?"

Thurman extended his free arm for her, and we walked up the stairs together.

Except for the organist playing a hymn, and a few coughs and occasional scuffling of feet, the church was hushed. The nave was divided in two, and we sat halfway up on the right side.

As the service got underway, I looked around the church. The family sat at the front on the left hand side. I saw the back of Gary's head. A strawberry blonde I guessed was Kamie sat to his right and Mildred sat beside her. Gary's mother and father sat to his left. Nathan's absence was more conspicuous than Mildred's hot pink blouse.

I didn't see Ariana or Dawson and wondered if they were blocked from view or if they hadn't come to the funeral. When the pastor asked the congregation to stand and sing *It Is Well with My Soul,* I took the opportunity to look behind me. Ariana and Dawson were two rows back across the aisle. Ariana wore one of her little black dresses. Dawson wore one of his little black suits. It seemed all was well with their souls, too. Dawson's arm encircled Ariana's waist as they shared a hymnal. They stood so close together, a communion wafer wouldn't slip between them.

The service was performed by a pastor who obviously knew only the Sunday side of Claire. It showed her in a good light, and at the end there was the usual invitation to be saved as the organist played *Just As I Am*. The pastor announced a private burial would be held at a later date, but the family had asked everyone to join them in the fellowship hall where the ladies of the church had prepared lunch.

We caught up to Ariana and Dawson holding hands on the way out of the church. They were headed away from the fellowship hall.

"You and Dawson seem more like bride and groom rather than mourners," I said.

Ariana glanced at her husband who grinned like a mule eating briars. "Are you going to explain the misunderstanding, my dear jealous wife?"

She pouted. "It's none of their business."

"I agree. But since they already know the beginning of your little drama, the least you can do is explain how it ends."

She looked at him for a few moments. "Do I have to?"

"I know you hate to admit when you're wrong." He folded his arms, stepped back, and waited.

When she realized he wouldn't give in and we weren't going away, Ariana said, "I spoke with Lily."

Willi's eyes flew open wide. "You called her?"

"She called me. Lily *is* Dawson's cousin. His mother's oldest sister's granddaughter. So I guess she's a second cousin or something like that. She works for a large agricultural products company and lives in Montana, that is before she was transferred to Waco. His mother volunteered Dawson to his aunt. She told his aunt that Dawson could help Lily get set up in Texas. He found Lily an apartment and put the deposit on a six-month lease, which she has already repaid. She's all moved in. And I don't like to say it, because I was enjoying hating her, but she seems like a very sweet girl. She's invited us to come visit."

"I told you Dawson was innocent."

"I would never have suspected otherwise if he had told me about Lily to begin with," she said begrudgingly.

"It slipped my mind," Dawson said.

"Well, I'm glad *that's* over with," I said. "Aren't y'all going to the fellowship hall?"

"I've got work to do," Dawson said.

Thurman said, "If we're going with them to Vegas, *I* have to go to work."

"Willemina, I wish you'd reconsider and go with us," Ariana said.

"I told you this morning, I'm busy with the Fall Awards Banquet; besides, I don't care anything about gambling."

"Shopping, Willemina, shopping. Lots and lots of shopping. The Forum Shops, the Canal Shops, the Bellagio Shops. Dolce and Gabana, Yves St. Laurent, Chanel."

I could see the battle going on inside Willemina. But the Volunteer-of-the-Year beat out the Shopper-of-the-Century. "I *cannot* plan a trip before next January. Besides the banquet for the Chamber of Commerce, I have committee meetings for two organizations right around the corner, and then there's Thanksgiving and Christmas, and you know what those are like at my house. Then there's

Richard's schedule. He would have to rearrange his calendar."

"Excuse me," Dawson said. "But may I interrupt?" He turned to Ariana. "We're going to Vegas?"

She wrinkled her nose. "I guess we have a few more things to discuss."

Dawson shook his head. "Let's discuss them on the way home."

I grabbed Ariana's hand. "Why don't you talk tonight? I need to borrow your wife this afternoon."

"What for?" Ariana asked.

"We haven't talked to Gary yet, and we probably won't have another chance to talk to Kamie."

"I have work to do."

"It won't take long."

"We need to get back, too," Thurman said.

"Willi can take Ariana and me home," I said. "Can't you, Willi?"

"Uh ... sure," she said.

Thurman gave me a hard look. "What are you up to?" Willemina and Ariana were looking at me with the same curiosity.

"I told you. We haven't had a chance to extend our sympathy to Gary and Kamie," I said.

He gave me an *I'll-bet* look. "You girls stay out of trouble."

That's what I was hoping to do. After all, how much trouble could we get into at church? "Bye, sweetheart. Bye, Dawson," I said as I nudged Willi and Ariana toward the fellowship hall.

Chapter Thirty-five

"What *are* you up to?" Willi asked.

We carefully made our way along the cracked sidewalk under the shade of the cottonwoods. Ariana and Willi walked side by side. I took up the rear.

"Why do y'all keep asking that? I told you. We haven't extended our sympathy to Gary and Kamie."

Willemina stopped and turned toward me. "Nonsense. You mean, we haven't had a chance to question Gary and Kamie."

"That, too."

Willi had stopped so fast Ariana was a few steps ahead of us. When she heard what Willi said, she turned back. "Questioning the survivors at the funeral is a bit insensitive, don't you think?"

"This may be the only chance we have," I said. "I'll talk to Gary and Kamie. Willi, you talk to Mildred. Ariana you—"

"Leave me out of it," she interrupted.

"You don't have to do anything except keep Victoria occupied."

"Who is Victoria?"

"I'll introduce you. If she says anything about Paul Newman, tell her it was *fabulous* working with him."

"I never worked with Paul Newman."

"Just go with the flow." I motioned for them to proceed ahead of me.

Ariana shook her head in annoyance but followed Willemina to the door of the fellowship hall. A line of people extended from the door to the buffet tables set up at the other end of the brisket-scented room. Other mourners were slowly filling up the folding chairs on either side of long rows of tables.

As we moved into the main hall from the foyer, we came face to face with Victoria Nathe. Victoria looked past Willi, glanced at me, and saw Ariana. She looked back at me, grabbed me as if I were a life raft thrown to her in a flash flood, and said, "Darby, darling. Thank you so much for coming." She released me then wept into a lace-trimmed hanky.

"Victoria, I'd like you to meet my friends," I said.

Willi held out her hand. "I'm Willemina Henry. I'm so very sorry about Claire."

"Thank you," she sniffed.

"Willemina is Dr. Richard Henry's wife," I said. "You know Dr. Henry, the *plastic surgeon.*"

Her tears dried up in a hurry. "Of course. Oh, *darling,* thank you for coming."

"And this," I said, waving my hand in a grand gesture, "is Ariana."

Victoria was speechless until Ariana stepped forward and extended her hand. Victoria hugged Ariana as if she'd known her all her life. "Thank you for coming. Thank you. Thank you." Ariana shot me a you-owe-me look over

Victoria's shoulder. Victoria stepped back and linked her arm through Ariana's. "You're so gracious to come to our little gathering." She glanced at Willi and me. "Excuse us," she said as she lead Ariana to the center of the room, sure to be seen by all.

"I've never thought of a funeral as a 'little gathering'," Willemina said.

"Unbelievable, isn't she?"

"Ariana is going to be quite put out with you. You know she doesn't like to bring attention to herself in situations like these."

"I know, but Victoria was dying to meet her, and Ariana provides a great distraction." The crowd of people who had been uniformly scattered around the room when we entered, suddenly began to gravitate toward Victoria and Ariana. Ariana was going to shoot me later, but I didn't want to spend this time playing her proxy for Victoria.

I scanned the room for the rest of the Nathes. It didn't take long. Mildred's hot pink advertised their position standing off to the side near a door opening to another part of the building. "Lead the way," I said.

Gary, Kamie, and Mildred stood side by side, and for an instant I saw them dressed like a row of soldiers—like a row of the Queen's guards lined up in front of Buckingham Palace.

Willemina and I waited as a tall man with a mustache shook hands with Gary, offered to help in any way he could, and moved on to shake hands with Kamie and Mildred in turn. Willi shook hands with Gary, offered her condolences, then introduced herself to Kamie.

"These are the ladies who stopped by the other day," Mildred said. She pointed to me. "I think you're the one that got Nathan so upset."

"I'm sorry," I said. "I was wrong."

"Damn right, you were wrong!" Kamie said, in a voice

that sounded eerily like her mother's. "You're the reason Nathan's in jail, you bitch."

I stepped back, wanting to run, but at the same time wanting to confront her.

"I understand how upset you are by all that has occurred, but—" Willi began.

"Shut up," Kamie spat. "You're as bad as she is. You both have a lot of nerve showing up today after what you said to Nathan."

"Kamie, please lower your voice," Gary said, the distress evident in his voice.

I noticed the din directly behind me had decreased and imagined more than a few eyes turned our way.

"I know Nathan didn't strangle your mother," I said.

"Then why did you accuse him?" Kamie said loudly, unmindful of her father. Nathan was close to his sister. I doubt he had talked to Mildred about what I'd said, so Kamie had to have heard my accusation through Nathan.

"Let's talk where it's a little more private," Willi said, gesturing toward the door.

I glanced behind me. There were *a lot* of people looking at us.

Gary seemed happy to get out of the earshot of others. He led the way, then Kamie, Mildred, Willemina, and I filed out the door and down a door-lined hallway. Gary opened the first door he reached, and we marched into a Sunday school room for the primary grades. Little chairs sat at little tables. Bulletin board cut-outs of smiling suns and clouds, angels, shepherds, and Jesus surrounded by children covered the walls.

Kamie turned to me. "Well? I'm waiting for an answer."

"You have every right to be angry with me," I said, stepping a few feet back and just to the left of the bulletin board, well out of Kamie's reach and closer to God, in case Kamie decided to get physical.

"I jumped to the wrong conclusion when I saw the picture of Nathan at the gala. I was looking for proof of Isaac's innocence." I turned to Gary. "Maybe you can clear it up for me, Gary. You asked Nathan to bring some equipment to the community center. Nathan said he wore a tuxedo for those few minutes to drop off a lens and filter just to keep from embarrasing Claire. That's hard for me to believe. I'd never expect my kids to go formal just to run an errand." I turned to Willi. "Would you? Would you expect Raven to put on an evening gown just to drop off something to you?"

"I'd be happy if she cleaned the paint off her face first."

"Exactly. If Nathan didn't rent a tuxedo for the sole purpose of blending in with the other patrons, where did he get it at such short notice?"

"From his closet," Gary said. "Claire convinced my mother to buy a tuxedo for Nathan for the prom."

"That's an expensive purchase for one prom."

"Claire told her Nathan would have many more occasions to use it when he became a prominent lawyer." *Prominent lawyer* came out very sarcastically. "I suggested he wear it. Claire would have thrown a.... Claire would have been disappointed in Nathan if he dressed inappropriately."

I turned when I heard the door open behind me. Ariana slipped into the room. She clicked the lock on the knob and stood directly in front of the vertical slit window of the door. I guessed she'd escaped and was blocking the view in case Victoria had followed her.

"And he didn't want to disappoint Claire," I said, turning back. "Nathan attempted to appease Claire from clothing to college. How did you feel about Nathan going to Harvard, Gary?"

Gary wore a look of utter sadness. "I wanted what he wanted."

"He wanted to go to MIT, but there wasn't enough

prestige in mathematics for Claire, was there? Just as there wasn't enough prestige in wildlife photography for her. How did she force you to give up your dream?"

Kamie walked to Gary's side. "She burned all of his work," Kamie said.

"You weren't even three years old," Gary said incredulously. "You remember?"

"How could I forget? She threw everything that was in your studio out the back door and set fire to it. I didn't understand what she had done until I was older, but I remembered it."

"Claire ran her business and yours, even to the point of firing your employees," Ariana said. "Why did you let her, Gary? Why did you let her frame Jaclyn?"

He shook his head. "I was afraid. I was afraid for Nathan. Claire hated Jaclyn because I liked her and because Nathan enjoyed working with her. Nathan started arguing with Claire about college. He told her he didn't want to go to Harvard. Claire blamed Jaclyn when Nathan stood up to her, but instead of punishing him directly, Claire punished Nathan through Jaclyn. She was gifted at indirect punishment."

"Like Kamie's cat?" I asked.

"How did you know about that?"

"I've been asking questions. I know Kamie left home when it happened. Why didn't you leave home, Gary? Why didn't you leave Claire?"

His voice was almost a whisper. "I wanted to. I wanted to leave her *before I married her.*"

I looked at Mildred. Hearing these things about her daughter didn't seem to surprise her. She looked back at me as if appraising me then walked over to the teacher's desk, pulled out the chair, and sat down.

"Then why did you marry her?" Kamie asked.

"She was pregnant—with you."

"You did the honorable thing, then stayed for the sake of the children," Willemina said.

"There were a lot of times I wanted to leave," Gary said. "But I knew better, especially after Kamie ran away. I told Claire I wanted a divorce, that I was taking Nathan and getting as far away from her as I could."

"Why didn't you?" I asked.

He shook his head but said nothing.

After a long moment Kamie spoke. "I'll tell you why." She looked over at her grandmother, then at Gary, then at me. "She told him she'd accuse him of child abuse. Nathan told me. He heard her screaming at Dad. She said she'd tell the police I ran away because Dad was sexually abusing me and Nathan. But it wasn't true. He never touched us."

Another false accusation that would be believed. "It was after Claire ruined J.D. Woodard's reputation. You knew she'd be believed. If not by the police, by the community. I understand why you wanted to kill Claire *then*," I said. "But you didn't. You didn't kill Claire when she destroyed your artwork. You didn't kill her when Kamie ran away. You didn't kill her when she framed Jaclyn. What were you waiting for?"

Chapter Thirty-six

"Leave him alone!" Kamie shouted.

Ariana spoke up. "Gary could have taken the belt that was used to strangle Claire. I told him he could find the guard's costume in the dressing room with the other clothes for the style show. He could have picked up the belt along with the costume, and no one would be the wiser."

"His fingerprints weren't on the belt. The police told us Isaac Molina's were. How do you explain that?" Kamie said.

"He could have used a scarf or gloves," Ariana said.

"Gloves," I said. "Photographers keep a supply. They don't want fingerprints on the pictures. But the pictures were the fingerprints in this case."

"What are you talking about?" Kamie asked.

"It's no use, Kamie." Gary stepped forward, showing the first sign of bravery I'd seen from him. "You're right. I killed Claire. I killed her because she had ruined my life, and she was trying to ruin my son's life. Nathan had nothing to do with the murder."

"Kamie did," Willemina said.

We all turned to gape at Willemina.

"You attended the gala," Willi said to Kamie. "You wore your hair up, so it took me a while to place you. But I saw you that night. You wore a black strapless Chloé knock-off. Nice dress by the way."

"Thanks," she said flatly.

"Did Nathan tell you about Isaac and Claire's fight?" I asked, "or was it your dad?" She said nothing, so I pressed on. "You stayed in contact with Nathan and your dad after you left. How was it your mother never found out?"

"Kamie called when she was sure her mother wasn't around," Gary said. "Kamie didn't do anything. It was *me*."

"Claire put Mildred through hell trying to find out Kamie's whereabouts. Surely she gave you the same trouble?"

"She hounded us for weeks," Gary said. "But we didn't know where Kamie was. Kamie wouldn't tell us. She sent a friend to tell me she was safe and that she'd contact me when she could."

"Patrick?"

Gary nodded.

"Kamie was protecting you," Willi said. She looked at me. "Gary could have killed Claire, Kamie could have killed Claire, and Nathan could have killed Claire. Now what do we do?"

"We also know Mildred was at the benefit," I said.

"We do?" Willi and Ariana asked in unison.

Mildred smiled. "I was afraid all those cameras going off were going to be trouble. *I* killed Claire."

Willi said, *"You killed your own child?"*

She shrugged. "It happens."

"You didn't wake up last Friday and decide to kill her!"

"I think it started a long time ago, didn't it, Mildred?" I asked. "You said when Claire stopped letting the children visit, 'it near about killed us.' Then when Kamie ran away,

Claire viciously harrassed you and your husband. What happened to Bernie?"

"Bernie died."

"*How* did he die?"

The jolly greeter's face contorted with anger. "He had a stroke. A massive stroke. I tried to keep the letters away from him. They worried him so. But I couldn't always get to the mailbox before Bernie did, and sometimes there would be four or five letters. Claire blamed us for Kamie running away. She sent newsclippings of horrible things that happened to runaways, murdered children, raped and sodimized. Horrible, horrible things that Bernie read, and it just ate at him. The stroke didn't kill him right away. He lingered for several years."

I looked at Kamie. Tears streamed down her face as her grandmother spoke. "You didn't contact your grandparents when you first ran away, because you didn't want your mother to find you through them. You didn't want to give her a reason to harrass them, either. But it didn't matter. Your mother was relentless." I wanted to reach out and give her a comforting hug, but the time for comfort was long past. "You couldn't save your grandfather. But you could save your brother. Is that what you did last Friday night? Save your brother? Did he call you and talk to you about Claire?"

She nodded. "He called me. She wasn't going to let him go to college. Not *any* college. She said he needed to forget about school. He was going to stay in Dulcinea and run the studio." With a mix of sadness and bitterness, she said, "Mother was afraid if he got too far away, she'd have no control over him or Dad."

"Kamie didn't do nothing," Mildred said, "except tell me where Claire was going to be." She stood up and leaned over the desk. "*I* killed Claire."

"Dios mio," Ariana said, stomping over to my side.

"Nathan killed Claire. Gary killed Claire. Kamie killed Claire. Mildred killed Claire. *Who in the hell killed Claire?*"

I looked around the room. Gary was staring at the floor. Kamie angrily wiped away tears. Mildred's face morphed back into the happy greeter. I looked at my two bewildered friends. "Ariana, you just told us," I said. "They all killed Claire."

Gary stepped forward. "*I killed Claire,*" he said angrily. "Leave them out of it. *I* did it."

Gary's bravado lasted only a moment. When he stepped back to sit on a nearby table, I said, "I believe you provided the murder weapon. Did you pick up the belt when Ariana told you where to find the guard's costume?"

He nodded. "I saw Isaac carry it into the dressing room earlier."

"He was the *poifect* patsy," Willi said in her bad B-movie accent. I glared at her. She shrugged and smiled in return. "Isaac had had an argument with Claire earlier in the day that was witnessed by a number of people, then he handled something that could be used as a murder weapon. It was *poifect.*"

"Then why did Nathan confess?" Ariana asked.

"Because Isaac was released from jail," I said. "Nathan *knew* Isaac didn't kill Claire. He assumed Isaac was released because there wasn't enough evidence to hold him. Nathan either strangled her himself, or he was confessing to protect one of you. In any case, Nathan wasn't alone. It was a family affair. That's why Kamie and Mildred came to Dulcinea." I turned to Gary. "You couldn't do it alone, could you? Otherwise, you would have done it a long time ago, long before Claire killed Kamie's cat or terrorized Mildred." Gary shriveled up like a paper flower caught in a rainstorm.

Ariana spoke again. "So either Nathan or Gary called Kamie and Mildred to tell them there was a golden opportunity to kill Claire and pin it on someone else."

None of them replied.

"Kamie, your mother must have felt faint when you appeared at the gala," Willemina said.

Kamie grinned wickedly.

Mildred stood up, walked around the desk, and stood beside Kamie. "Not as shocked as she was to see me—there in the middle of all her society friends—all dressed up in my waitress outfit."

Kamie laughed. "The expression on Mother's face when she saw Gran was priceless. But Gran didn't kill my mother. I did. I told her she could go outside to talk about Nathan's college plans, or she could introduce me and Gran to all her friends."

"How did you get to the arena without anyone seeing you together?" Ariana asked.

"I waited until they announced the style show. I knew everyone's attention would be on the runway. It only took a moment to convince Mother she didn't want anyone to meet her waitress mom and hotel manager daughter—not when she'd told everyone in town that I was a Hollywood big shot. When the lights dimmed, I presented myself to Mother, then led her to the arena."

Gary, Kamie, and Mildred stood side by side. The image of the Queen's guard popped into my head. "Where the rest of the family were waiting," I said.

"So," Ariana said. "Which one of you tightened the belt around Claire's neck?"

"I did," they all said in unison.

A loud, persistant rapping, caused us to turn toward the door. Victoria's rabid-fan face was pressed against the six-inch wide glass. She jiggled the doorknob, and mouthed *let me in.*

Ariana took a deep breath, walked over to the door, and opened it.

"There you are, Ariana," Victoria said cheerfully. "I've been looking all over for you." She glanced over and saw Kamie. "I see you met my granddaughter," she said brightly. "She works with a famous director in Hollywood. Kamie, tell Ariana all about it."

Chapter Thirty-seven

The next night, Thurman and I drove to Ray's Pigskin to meet the gang for dinner. As we walked in, someone began to clap. Soon the whole room was applauding and looking our way. At first, I thought it was because I had helped solve a murder, but soon the laughter was as loud as the applause. Sitting on a bar stool, innocently drinking a soda, was Deputy Chuck Dechert. I felt myself go as red as the bottom of the Texas flag.

Ray stepped out from behind the bar, grinning like a king-size fool. He walked over to shake hands with Thurman and loudly announce, "take a victory lap, little brother." Thurman made a sweeping bow, to even louder applause, then circled the room giving high-fives to every man within reach, including Chuck, which brought on even more laughter.

Debbie sidled up next to me. "You ought to be ashamed of yourself acting like a dog-in-heat. That's an awful way for a nun's mother to behave. What would Marissa think?"

I looked at Debbie, thought about it a minute, then said, "I don't know what she'd think, but I know what she's missing." I jogged away, met Thurman on the turn, and gave him a big, juicy kiss. We walked hand in hand, accompanied by more applause and laughter, to the table where Richard, Willemina, Dawson and Ariana awaited. I sat across from Willemina and next to Ariana. Thurman sat beside me.

"You are embarrasing," Ariana said when we sat down.

Dawson reached over and took her hand. "After the night and morning we had, *I* deserve a victory lap myself."

Ariana blushed, but a slow, sultry grin spread across her face.

We all broke up laughing.

Ariana waved her free hand. "*¡Cállense!*" She waited until we were quiet, then asked, "What's going to happen to the Nathes?"

I shrugged. "I guess they'll all be charged in one way or another. After all, it *was* a conspiracy. I'm glad I won't have to sit on the jury, because I'd have a hard time convicting any of them."

"They committed murder, Darby," Willi said. "You're the reason they're in jail. The investigation was your idea."

"I know. But I feel sorry for all of them."

Willemina shook her head and looked toward heaven as if asking God to knock some sense into me.

"Who did the actual killing?" Dawson asked.

"Kamie," Willi said. "She didn't fall too far from the tree. She showed no remorse for Claire's murder. But—she felt guilty for leaving her father and brother behind when she ran away. That guilt is what pushed her to come back and kill Claire."

"I think it was Mildred," Ariana said.

"I know she confessed, but I don't care what she said. I don't see how anyone could kill their own daughter."

"It happens somewhere in this world every day."

"It wasn't Mildred. Did you see her hands?" I asked.

"Arthritis," Willi said.

"Yes. Mildred has enough strength in her arms, because she's spent a lifetime carrying heavy trays, but she probably has trouble opening a ketchup bottle. I don't believe she could grip a belt. But it was a consorted effort. They all wanted Claire dead. Mildred blamed Claire for causing her beloved Bernie's stroke. And Gary knew he'd never be free of her."

"Gary provided the murder weapon. Kamie and Mildred lured Claire to the arena," Thurman said. "Where does Nathan fit in?"

"He planned it," I said.

"WHAT?" they all shouted.

"Sweet, subservient Nathan?" Ariana asked.

"Sweet, subservient Nathan never had a reason to disobey Claire before. There may have been minor things he wanted to challenge her on, but he was conditioned to accept her demands or pay the price. There wasn't anything he wanted badly enough—until college."

"You're saying the kid was the mastermind behind the murder?" Dawson said.

"He set it in motion by calling Kamie and telling her Claire was pulling the college rug out from under him. He wanted to spend his life studying mathematics. He wanted to attend MIT. He has a mathematical, systematic mind. He knew his sister felt guilty for leaving him behind. He knew Gary felt trapped *and* felt guilty for Claire trapping *him.* All Nathan had to do was say the right thing at the right time to the right person and the wheels would continue to spin."

"He confessed. How's he going to talk his way out of it?"

"He won't. He knows Gary, Kamie, and Mildred will do their utmost to take the heat off him and put it on themselves."

"That boy planned it all?" Willi asked. "Well, it is the quiet ones you've got to watch out for," she said, glancing toward Richard.

On the day of Claire's funeral, when Thurman had used the phrase to refer to Nathan, it had not sounded as accusatorial as it did coming from Willemina. Her teasing remark made me very uncomfortable since I now knew of Richard's past infidelity. I was glad when Ariana asked me, "How did you know Mildred was at the gala. Was she in one of the photos you took?"

I shook my head. "I was bluffing."

"Bluffing!" Ariana said, doubtfully. "Are you sure it wasn't your *bu—*"

"I was bluffing," I interrupted. Maybe I bluffed because of what I felt at Claire's house, or because of Mildred's comments about her daughter, or because of the picture of the Queen's guard.

A *coup d'état.* The overthrow of Queen Claire by her family. Maybe it was a combination that led me to believe Mildred was a part of the conspiracy. I didn't know or care why I bluffed, but I didn't want Ariana using the term *bug guts.*

"It was a good bluff," Willemina said, plucking the lemon from the side of her glass and squeezing it into her iced tea. "You know, we never got around to choosing a name for our little detective agency."

I gestured to my husband. "Thurman did."

Willi looked at him questioningly.

"I did what?" he asked.

"He called us the meddling *amigas.*"

Richard and Dawson laughed. But Ariana and Willi didn't see the humor; they both frowned.

Richard clapped his hands and rubbed them together, then his big bass voice boomed out, "Enough of this. Let's get down to business. When are we going to Vegas?"

"Vegas?" Willemina asked. "We can't go to Vegas. I already discussed it with Ariana."

"You didn't discuss it with *me*," he said.

Willi began listing all the reasons she couldn't possibly go to Las Vegas with all the events she had to coordinate, but I lost focus of what she was saying when a wave of *afterglow* hit.

Afterglow is another feeling I get. It's essentially the opposite of *bug guts*. You know the feeling you get when your heart swells with so much love for someone it hurts? Maybe you've felt it when you were holding your lover after making love, or when you look down at your baby after you rocked him to sleep, or when you finally realized you love someone enough to truly "forgive and forget." That is what *afterglow* is like. And when it's really, really strong, it makes me cry. It hits when something wonderful is going to happen.

"Damn it, Willemina," Richard was saying. If I can cancel surgery, you can get someone to handle your events."

"Richard, it isn't as easy as—"

"Willemina," I interrupted, wiping away the tears. "Say yes. Take your husband to Las Vegas."

She noticed my blotchy face and red eyes and leaned forward. "Are you crying?"

I shook my head. "Allergies." I enlaced my fingers and rested my chin on my folded hands like an innocent little angel saying her prayers. "I'll help you with the African American Chamber of Commerce banquet, *as long as* you won't recruit me for another event until—until Raven's wedding."

She leaned back in her chair. "*Raven's wedding?* You want to stop volunteering all together, don't you?"

I smiled in answer.

"All right. We'll go to Las Vegas." She shook her finger at me. "But don't expect me *not* to ask for your help before

Raven gets married. As anti-marriage as my daughter is, that day may never arrive."

I leaned back in my chair and smiled as Willemina's anti-marriage daughter and her boyfriend walked up to the table to join us for dinner. Raven kissed her mother on the cheek. James shook hands with Richard.

I love weddings.

Dancing at the Shoulder of the Bull
by Laramee Douglas

The ranch is a world away from the drugs and gangs of Houston, but even on his own turf, John Suarez can't shake the image of the dead child.

In the darkness of the bedroom, Ranita Hunter reaches for the phone futilely praying the caller is her husband. Her hello is met by silence.

Murder throws John back into police work and into the company of the woman he spent fifteen years avoiding. But Ranita needs his help, whether she wants it or not. Letters threatening Ranita and her family begin to arrive, and while John races to discover the identity of the stalker, the threat grows to real danger, and even running home to Daddy can't save Ranita and her children from the killer.

"Dancing at the Shoulder of the Bull
is Laramee Douglas' first novel
and makes interesting reading.
The mysterious side to the novel functions well,
with Douglas creating
various motives and interesting ideas."
--Bookideas.com

"Slick prose, standard situations, and personal tensions;
recommended."
--Library Journal

Alligator Tree Press
P. O. Box 4988
Victoria, TX 77903

Alligator Tree Press

www.alligatortree.com